BLOOD MOON

Soham P. Shah

Om Books International

Soham P. Shah's career in advertising and film-making spans a period of around twenty-six years.

A commercial arts graduate of Sir JJ School of Art, Mumbai, he launched an advertising company, Able & Will, in 1994 and went on to craft impactful campaigns for top-tier clients in the corporate world as well as the Indian film industry.

After assisting well-known film-makers Karan Johar and Ram Gopal Varma in *Kabhi Khushi Kabhi Gham* (2001) and *Bhoot* (2003) respectively, Shah made his directorial debut with *Kaal* (2005) and followed it with the action-thriller *Luck* (2009).

Among his upcoming projects are the psychological drama *Kartam Bhugtam* (slated for release in 2024) and an exhibition of his mythological paintings. *Blood Moon* marks his first foray into literary writing, blending his two loves: the written word and the supernatural.

Praise for the Book

"Sometimes you read a novel and you end up feeling that I want to see this on the big screen. *Blood Moon* gave me just that vibe. I could visualise the frames, feel the sound treatment in Soham's writing. I am sure the world will see this as visual content soon."

—Vivek Anand Oberoi, actor

"It's scary, it's unique, it's eerie, it's new-age, it's out of the box and it's also emotional. I was hooked and could imagine the characters coming alive. Stunning."

—Karan Singh Grover, actor

"Matheran, a family, a haunted hotel, a restless spirit, a perfect recipe for a ghost story. There have been many ghost stories, but Soham has cracked a new approach to the genre. It's sharp, it's fast-paced, it's edgy and most importantly, it's relatable."

—Shreyas Talpade, actor

"Soham Shah is a storyteller, be it through his films or now his first novel. The premise itself is so intriguing that you will want to start reading it right away. Be warned, you will not want to keep the book down before completing it. And I mean it. Happy chills and thrills, shrieks and screams!"

—Komal Nahta, film trade analyst

"Soham Shah's first step in writing a thriller is surefooted and atmospheric. His instinctive eye as a keen photographer, his imaginative creativeness as a graphics designer and his cinematic knack as a film-maker come together to create a vivid narrative. A fast-paced and compulsive read."

—Bharathi S. Pradhan, senior journalist and author

First published in 2024 by

Om Books International

Corporate & Editorial Office
A-12, Sector 64, Noida 201 301
Uttar Pradesh, India
Phone: +91 120 477 4100
Email: editorial@ombooks.com
Website: www.ombooksinternational.com

Sales Office
107, Ansari Road, Darya Ganj,
New Delhi 110 002, India
Phone: +91 11 4000 9000
Email: sales@ombooks.com
Website: www.ombooks.com

ISBN: 978-81-960433-9-1

Printed in India

10 9 8 7 6 5 4 3 2 1

Contents

1

The Turning Point

The shrill ring of the alarm jolts him out of his dream with a sound that has grown tiresomely familiar over the years. But today, it is with a feeling of anticipation rather than irritation that Manish Shah hits the snooze button with a practised hand.

Slowly, as is his habit, he awakens to his surroundings without opening his eyes. The morning chill alerts him to the fact that he is not sweating through an October heatwave in Mumbai. He feels an instant relief and then realisation dawns.

They are still on a family vacation, 83 km away, in Matheran, though today is the last day of their week-long Diwali break. By this time tomorrow, Manish will be back in the city, juggling responsibilities thrust on him by the family business. With a groan, he burrows deeper under the covers, wishing he could sleep in forever.

The alarm cuts into his thoughts. Chetna, his wife, stirs restlessly beside him, incoherently grumbling as she pulls the covers over her head to block out the sound of Bad Company's "Shooting Star" that her husband has selected as his alarm ringtone. Not wanting to get an earful first thing in the morning, Manish jumps up and turns off the alarm with one quick swipe. "Sorry, baby! Didn't mean to wake you. *So jao*. It's still early."

Chetna had carefully drawn the curtains before going to bed last night to blot out the sunlight in the morning. But a few weak rays now steal in through the skylights cut high in the walls, illuminating their bedroom in Dune Barr House.

Their bed is an old-world mahogany four-poster. This and the other furniture in the room—mirrored double almirah, antique writing table, straight-backed chair, intricately carved bedside table and red velvet-covered loveseat by the bay window—take him back to his hostel days in Shimla. Those were the golden days of his youth and the memories remain vivid. Perhaps that's why he makes annual visits to this heritage property in the picturesque hill station of Matheran even though the trails around the place are still rough and it's a long way off from the railway station and the bustling market on Mall Road. The service and food are, however, excellent—even for Chetna's exalted standards.

For Manish, this resort, tucked deep in a thicket and far removed from the busy hum of the main town, is an oasis of serenity even with the boys around. The efficient staff manages to keep them engaged with all kinds of activities, giving Chetna time to catch up on her OTT shows and him a chance to finish some much-needed paperwork. But today, he has promised to take his sons to Sunrise Point, with twelve-year-old Avinash sitting alone on a horse for the first time.

As if on cue, there is a polite knock on the door. Slipping his feet into a pair of mules, Manish pads to it and cracks it open. The boy facing him is in his early twenties, personable with an affable smile on his face despite the unearthly hour. "Good morning, sir. I hope you slept well. Sorry to disturb you but the horses are here and you would not want to miss out on the sunrise, I guess," he says in a soft, pitch-perfect voice. Manish smiles his appreciation, saying, "I will be down in fifteen minutes."

The boy melts away into the still dark passageway, while Manish returns to the bedside table to groggily peer down at his phone. It is just past five in the morning. Raking a hand through his hair, which is calling out for a salon trim, he disappears into the bathroom, shivering as the early-morning chill penetrates through the thick tee he had worn to bed.

Five minutes later, he steps out, all traces of sleep washed away. His choice of trendy athleisure defines the muscles in his six-foot frame, the result of five punishing days of hour-long workouts every week. He stands in front of the floor-length mirror and preens, a frown creasing his brow as he notices the not-too-visible bulge of fat settling in his middle-aged middle. He pinches it between his fingers distastefully, wondering if he should go for liposuction. Just exercise and diet are obviously no longer enough.

"Why are you looking at yourself for so long? Do you have an early-morning date?" Chetna's gruff, sleep-laced voice makes him smile. Her eyes are peeking out from over the covers, lit up with laughter.

"I wish. But even if I manage to get away from you for a couple of hours, the boys are there to spy on me," he complains with a pretend scowl.

"You were the one who wanted them underfoot," she reminds him. Then, with worry wrinkling her face, she throws aside the covers and sits up. "Manish, are you sure it's safe for Avi to ride alone? He's only twelve, still a baby. You know how..."

Her husband's response is firm and reassuring. "Now let us not go down that road again, Chetna. I promise, I will bring both Avinash and Aashu back to you, safe and sound and a little scruffy, all in time for the four of us to sit down to breakfast together. Now sleep, baby. It's only a few minutes past five."

Grumbling about how he never listens to her, Chetna lies down again, her head disappearing under the comforter as Manish tiptoes out into the corridor. Knocking on the door opposite their room, he stands wondering how to haul his boys out of bed when the door is flung open by Avi, who is already dressed and buzzing with excitement. "Are the horses here already?" he asks.

Manish nods and his son does a little jig that makes him laugh. He then asks if Aashu is up and his fifteen-year-old first-born replies from inside, "Just lacing up my sneakers, dad." Manish shakes his head in disbelief.

Suddenly, Avi slides up to him and anxiously whispers, "Dad, you don't think the horse will throw me off, do you?"

Manish laughs and ruffles his son's hair. "I don't expect he will. But just so he feels kindly towards you, maybe you can feed him a carrot or two and a few lumps of sugar before we set out. That way he will be a friend."

"That's a good idea, but what if he..." Avi breaks off abruptly as Aashu, a younger version of their dad, steps out momentarily.

Realising that Avi doesn't want to appear scared before Aashu, whom he idolizes, Manish completes the sentence. "Your brother was just suggesting that it might be a good idea to take along some treats for the horses."

Aashu nods approvingly. "Yes, they would like that." Avi beams with pride.

***

Together, the trio walks into the reception area with its stained-glass skylight panels and cathedral-like high ceiling. There's always a tranquil feeling about the place, more so at this particular hour as the other guests are still asleep. Most of them are elderly couples, given that the place is rather expensive compared to the other lodges. They will set off for their morning walks in about an hour.

There's a lone receptionist sitting at the desk, who is waiting for his colleague to relieve him after an uneventful and lonesome night shift. He is glad to chat with Manish and the boys, who are courteous and smiling. When he learns from Avinash, who can barely stand still, that he will be riding alone for the first time, Sanjay is happy to call for carrots and sugar cubes from the kitchen.

Carrying the packet, Avi runs to the gate where the horses are pacing restlessly, held down by a boy of around twenty who looks like he could do with a good bath. His warm grin welcomes Avi, and before long, Rashid is showing the boy how to hold out a carrot for his gentle mare, Bijli, to nibble on.

For a few minutes, Aashu stands beside his dad, trying to appear cool and grown-up, before he gives up the pretence and sets out to befriend his own horse, Chetak, with some sugar cubes.

A wizened man of around sixty is sitting on a boulder a short distance away and puffing on a bidi. He slowly pulls himself to his feet and walks up to Manish. Smiling at the boys, he says, "Don't worry, sahab. Rashid and I will make sure the young babas are safe. We know you can ride, so I didn't bother getting Arshad along."

Manish's chest puffs up with pride. Tilting his head in the direction of his sons, he says, "I started riding when I was younger than them. It's because of the horses that I come to Matheran every year. Your bhabhi-ji has finally agreed to let

Avinash ride alone, and I can bet you, Rahim chacha, he hasn't slept a wink last night. He's that excited."

The elderly horseman cackles, showing *gutka*-stained teeth, many of which are missing. "I promise after today, you will not be able to keep him away from horses," he says to assure Manish. Walking over to the horses, he starts rattling off brisk instructions to his son to saddle them up for the children.

Manish takes a moment to breathe in the unpolluted mountain air, knowing that soon he will be inhaling noxious carbon fumes in the city. The forest around him is shrouded in a silvery grey mist and looks like a beautiful painting. Somewhere close by, he can hear monkeys chattering. The birdsong makes him smile. It's so peaceful that he can almost believe he is in another world.

Turning behind, he strides up to a familiar black stallion. Bingo is stamping his hoofs, impatient to be gone. They have taken many rides together in the past, and with the ease of an experienced horseman, Manish hauls himself up and runs a gentle hand over the horse's mane to settle it down. Rahim watches him and nods approvingly—sahab knows his horse.

Bingo, Manish tells him, is surprisingly skittish this morning. The old man nods, stating, "Yes, he has not been himself since..." He breaks off abruptly. Manish is too caught up in the moment to prod. He smiles at the ghodawallah, confident that he will be able to manage the horse.

The boys are sitting astride their horses. Manish trots up and hands over his cellphone to Rashid, asking him to click a picture of them together. "Bhaiya-ji, *esmile*," the delighted boy earnestly says to Aashu, who is trying to look bored.

Rashid reminds Manish of the hired photographer who had followed Sonu Sood's Chhedi Singh in the Bollywood blockbuster *Dabangg*. "He used the exact same words," he recalls. Manish has no doubt that that's the cinematic moment from which the ghodawallah has picked up the phrase. The locals are avid Bollywood buffs, often plying him with questions about Salman Khan, Shah Rukh Khan, Deepika Padukone and Alia Bhatt. They feel disappointed that despite living in the same city, Manish has never met them.

As the boys set off at a canter, with Rahim and Rashid leading the horses, Manish takes a minute to upload the picture on his Instagram handle. He then posts it on Facebook and texts it to the family WhatsApp group for good measure. The caption reads, "The last ride."

Then, with a light slap on Bingo's flank, he sets off, easily catching up with the others. As they make their way up towards Sunrise Point, sunlight filters in through the surrounding dense foliage, lighting up the muddy path below. The ground is strewn with leaves, remains of the storm that blew in last evening and brought a nip in the air, hinting towards a fast-approaching winter.

Manish zips up his puffer jacket with one hand all the way up to the neck and loudly instructs his sons to do the same. That they don't argue tells him that they are feeling the chill too. It is quiet; only the occasional cry of an animal or a bird and the clip clop of the horses' hooves can be heard. They amble along, entranced by the view.

After a few minutes, Manish digs in his heels and picks up the pace. "See you on the other side of the mountain, boys. Love you," he shouts in a carefree tone as he gallops past them, with the wind in his hair and the sun in his eyes. Rashid's voice follows him, a trifle worried. "Sahab, take the right turn to Sunrise Point. The left goes up to Garbett Point. That road is closed, so don't go that way."

Manish hears him but doesn't bother to respond. Being out in the open is so liberating and such a rush. He can't see another human being for miles ahead. For a short while, he wants to enjoy the thrill of being absolutely alone. This kind of 'me time' is rare and therefore precious. Seventy-two hours from now, he will be back in his claustrophobic office, surrounded all day by people and their demands. It's good to make money—indeed he makes a lot of it—but he needs something to hold on to till the next trip, which will not happen before the next summer.

Rashid, however, refuses to be silent. "Sahab, don't miss the right turn. The horses get jittery near Garbett. It's not safe." The boy is beginning to exasperate Manish now. After all, he has been coming to Matheran for over a decade and must have been to Sunrise Point more than a hundred times. Who did the boy think he was, telling him where to go and how to get there? As if he would get lost, and even if he did, well, good riddance!

Still, Manish slows down, waiting for the others to catch up with him. Avi, he notices, is looking a little pale. He debates whether or not to let him walk up the rest of the way but then decides that he can't be a baby all his life. He needs to toughen up for the challenges life will bring along, thinks Manish. It's a pity that he is not a natural athlete like his brother and his father. The horsemen are being paid good money to make sure that he is safe.

Aashu, who is a born rider, is sitting up straight on his horse. No signs of nerves there. Manish shoots him a half smile before turning arrogantly towards Rashid, who is leading Avi's horse, the reins loosely wrapped around his hand. Raking him with a searing glance from head to toe, he asks, "How old are you, son?"

Rashid looks surprised by the question but answers with his usual cheeky grin. "*Pata nahi*, sahab. We don't cut birthday cakes here."

His father, who is walking alongside, adds, "*Hoga bees, baayees saal ka*, sahab. I have six sons and four daughters. It's difficult to remember when each was born."

Manish looks down at Rashid and retorts, "*Beta, jitna umar tera hai na, utne saal se ghode dauda raha hoon main.* I have been riding since I was twelve, over a decade in Matheran alone. I know every nook and cranny, every Point and peak here, so don't worry about me. I know how to take care of myself. You take care of my *bachchas*."

The boy understands immediately that he is being reprimanded but stubbornly says, "Sahab, I know you are familiar with this place and the horses, but since the pandemic, strange things have been happening here. Particularly on the road to Garbett and near the railway tracks. So, it's important that you don't miss the turn and..."

Before he can complete his sentence, Manish is off on a snorting Bingo, racing away with his head held high. Within minutes, he disappears from their view. Rashid looks at his father with concern. With an imperceptible nod, Rahim indicates that he should focus his attention on Avi. With a shrug, the boy turns away, but his eyes are clouded with worry as they scan the road ahead for the man and the stallion.

Aashu is looking around him and is not reassured by what he sees. The mountain to their right rises steeply and the soil is loose, occasionally sending down a shower of stones and dirt. What if there's a landslide? He shivers at the thought of being buried alive in the rubble.

On the right, the dirt road falls away into a treacherous ravine. He can see a streak of silver, which must be a river way below. What if someone fell down there? He has a sudden vision of a broken body lying in a pool of blood—hands and legs askew and the head tilted at an unnatural angle. Its eyes are wide open but unseeing, with an expression of fear frozen on the face. The visage seems familiar, yet Aashu can't recognize it. Corpses turn people into strangers. As he vigorously shakes his head to rid himself of the disturbing image, his eyes lock with Rahim chacha's. There is a hint of foreboding, as if the old man just peeked into his mind and read his thoughts.

Turning his head away resolutely, the teenager looks into the distance and strains for a glimpse of his father. He's nowhere to be seen. All he can see is the muddy trail, red and raw, that is taking them to a place high up on the hill from where they will see the day break. He would have been quite happy to watch the sunrise from his hotel, but dad liked him to do the things he himself enjoyed.

He can hear him saying, "Tennis at the club from Monday to Thursday, Aashu. No, don't whine. It's good for the legs, beta. And you are coming bowling with me on Saturday. You have a strong arm; it must be put to better use than watching a movie on your laptop. Sundays are for swimming. No, no excuses. You can chat with your friends later. The exercise will do you good. On this trip to Matheran, I want you to get really comfortable on a horse so that from next year onwards, you and I can go riding alone. Maybe Avi can accompany us if he turns out to be a natural rider like us. Together, we can watch the night melt away and the day break."

Attuned to his thoughts, Rahim chacha says something softly, his voice a whisper in the wind. "End of a dark night or the beginning of one?" He isn't usually so pessimistic, but life has been difficult since Covid-19, which robbed his family of their livelihood for over a year. The memory of those dismal months—being confined to the shacks and watching helplessly as his mother contracted the deadly virus and passed away—hasn't faded still.

Also, there was that incident at Cecil. He shudders as he remembers and quickly wrenches his mind from meandering in that direction.

Up ahead, Manish's horse suddenly tosses his head in the air and neighs. Taken by surprise, he digs his heels in and wonders what has set Bingo off. He can't see anybody. Disconcerted and distracted, he lets the horse choose which direction to take when the road forks.

Bingo takes the left turn. They go a few hundred yards up the hill when Manish realises the mistake. "Shit! We are going up to Garbett!" he exclaims.

Garbett Point is located in the south-west region of Matheran and offers a breathtaking view of the plateau at 2,600 feet above sea level. It's usually a medium-easy trek, and he's been up there several times on previous visits before the lockdowns were enforced. But today, something doesn't feel right. Suddenly and inexplicably, Manish breaks out in a cold sweat and turns to look over his shoulder. There's no one there.

Bingo picks up the pace and turns the corner.

2

The Woman on the Tracks

Manish tightens the reins, desperately trying to hold the horse back. But Bingo is suddenly the master and will not be overpowered. He races up the hill at a furious pace, coming to an abrupt halt as their path is blocked by a board hanging from a rusted chain tethered between two trees.

It is broken, undoubtedly the handiwork of the monkeys bounding around. Manish can hear a few of them chattering high up in the trees. He is glad that he had handed over his binoculars to Rahim chacha and wouldn't have to play tug-of-war with the monkeys now. He peers shortsightedly at the board. It is streaked with dust and dirt but he can still make out the word 'DANGER' scrawled in red.

He is seriously concerned now, wishing he had been more mindful of Rashid's repeated warnings and not behaved like a know-it-all idiot.

"Humpty Dumpty sat on a wall. Humpty Dumpty had a great fall," recites a soft voice in his ear, leading the hair at the nape of his neck to rise as the familiar nursery rhyme is made eerier by a mocking laugh punctuating it.

"Who's there?" Manish asks loudly, turning to look over his shoulder. There's no one, but jolted by the tone of his voice and the undercurrent of fear lacing it, Bingo takes off again, straining against the reins holding him back.

The horse gallops furiously down the hill as if the devil were after them, causing Manish to lose his balance. As the latter hangs sideways from the saddle, watching the earth rush up to swallow him whole, he sees his whole life flash before his eyes.

He can hear Chetna telling him that it is not enough just to make money. "We need to make some memories too; we don't have enough of them, Manish. What if one fine day it is suddenly all over for one of us. What will the boys remember us by then?" she once asked in a gently admonishing voice. In retrospect, he realises now that this was perhaps why, against her better judgement, she had agreed to let their sons ride with him this morning so that they could make some memories together. He remembers how worried she had been about Avi.

And like a fool, instead of staying with my sons and breaking Avi in gently, I set out to show them what a champ I am, he thinks, kicking himself mentally.

Then, just when he thinks this is the end for Manish Shah of Shah & Shah Enterprises, he hears Aashu say from somewhere close behind him, "No, dad, don't give up just yet. I need you… We all do." And with superhuman effort, Manish manages to haul himself up and regain his perch. But he is still unable to control the horse. Bingo is on fire, rushing down at a breathless pace and turning a deaf ear to his pleas to stop.

A shower of soil and stones rains down in the wake of the horse's reckless flight, leaving Manish trembling as the memory of a landslide in Shimla returns to haunt him. Years ago, in the eighth standard, he had gone on a class excursion and been surprised by a landfall which had swept away one of his teachers and a few classmates. He realises now that the past one thinks one has buried remains with them till the last breath.

Shivering uncontrollably, he wonders if he will meet with the same fate. What if he falls into the ravine and goes rolling all the way down? Will anyone find his body? Will there be anything left of him? Would they declare him missing and freeze all his accounts?

***

Meanwhile, Aashu and Avi have reached Sunrise Point with the ghodawallahs. A queasy Avi disembarks with a sense of relief, praying that he will not embarrass himself by throwing up. If his dad was around, he could have asked him to take him below into the trees so that he could be sick away from prying eyes. But there is no sign of Manish. He seems to have vanished into thin air! Avi shivers as a gust of wind blows.

Aashu is looking out at the mountains, which are beautifully serene in the reddish glow of the rising sun. The chirping birds and the dewy mist enhance the magic of the moment. He has seen the sunrise many times, yet it never fails to enchant him. But today, he can't seem to enjoy it. Rashid slides up to him and says with the air of a knowledgeable tourist guide, "Everyone calls this Sunrise Point but *isse* Panorama Point *bhi kehte hai bhai. Aur* Sunset Point is called Porcupine Point..."

Aashu grins back at him, saying, "Panorama Point *toh samajh mein aata hai* as it's quite a view from up here but Porcupine is a rather prickly term for a picture-perfect location like Sunset Point." Rashid laughs in agreement.

For once, Avi is not dancing around him, trying to butt into his conversations. He turns to see his younger brother looking back at the trail and watching a few trekkers make their way up. Aashu knows that he's wondering what's keeping their father. So is he.

The same thought is bothering Rahim as well. Sitting on one of the boulders and lighting up the half-smoked bidi, the ghodawallah admits to himself that sahab should have been here before them, given how fast he was going. "I hope he hasn't taken the wrong turn and gone up to Garbett," he mutters under his breath.

***

Bingo is like an animal possessed as he races down the hill. Manish is relieved when they finally hit plain ground even though the horse is still running. He lets out the breath he has been holding, knowing he has survived a free fall.

"The boys must be worried wondering what has happened to me. I have to get this damn horse under control and make my way up to them. If Avi gets spooked, it will be impossible to get him on a horse again," mumbles Manish. Suddenly, the honking of the approaching mini train breaks into his thoughts. He frowns; the first train doesn't arrive before 8 a.m. The horse raises his head, snorts and heads straight in the direction of the railway station. "No Bingo…Not that way…No…Noooo," screams Manish, with the wind snatching away his words. The echo of Rashid's voice reminds him of the danger ahead. "Slow down, boy. Slow down," he entreats as they round another blind turn, with rocks skittling.

There's a forest ahead of them. The horse crashes straight into the dark thicket. The trees stand close together and the branches hang low, slapping hard against his head as Bingo gallops through them. Monkeys jump out of his way, chattering and cowering in fright. Manish wishes he could swing from the branches like them but doesn't dare, afraid that if he tried to act like Tarzan, he might break every bone in his body. In fact, he might do so regardless if the damn horse doesn't stop.

They come out of the trees and are back on the road. Up ahead are the railway tracks. The train is getting closer. It must have entered the tunnel by now. Within minutes, it will emerge into view. Manish closes his eyes and prays fervently. "*Jai Shri Krishna*, save me this once and I promise I will never ride again."

***

Back in the hotel, Chetna is roaming about the bedroom restlessly. She is bathed and dressed. For some reason, she couldn't go back to sleep after Manish left with the boys. Something is bothering her but she can't put a finger on it.

The phone rings and she snatches it up, slightly disappointed that it's her mother-in-law and not her husband at the other end. "*Jai Shri Krishna,* Baa. No, you didn't wake me. I was up already…Yes, we will be leaving around 4 p.m. today…If the traffic isn't too bad, we should be home by dinner…No, Aashu and Avi are not around; they have gone riding with their father…Yes, even I am worried about Avi but you know how obdurate Manish can get sometimes… They left a little after five…They should be back by eight, in time for breakfast…No, we haven't spoken; the network here is terrible…I tried a few times and couldn't get through… Don't worry, Baa. Manish is a skilled rider and there are two ghodawallahs with them; they will be fine…Yes, yes, I will make sure to call you once they are back...Okay, Baa. You take care. We will be home soon."

***

Bingo is unstoppable as he charges towards the railway tracks. Manish narrows his eyes to slits, expecting to see the train rush in their direction. Instead he sees something that turns his blood cold. The horse has seen it too and comes to an abrupt stop. Rearing up on its hind legs, Bingo neighs in terror.

Manish wonders what the woman in front is doing crawling along the railway tracks with a train coming up any moment. He tries to yell a warning but no words come out. She struggles to her feet, holding something in her hands and clutching it to her breast. Then, as he watches horrified, she stumbles and falls. Scrabbling, she tries to rise, reaching for the parcel, and falls flat on her face. The train comes out of the tunnel, bearing down on her now. It's the scariest thing Manish has ever seen.

He tries one last time to get Bingo to stop but the horse has taken off towards Garbett, as if fleeing from what is to happen. They enter the thicket again. Manish is clinging on to the horse for dear life as he goes crashing through the foliage. When they emerge, a hanging branch hits him on the head, knocking him off the horse. This time, he falls to the ground, his head hitting a rock.

As he lies there lifelessly, blood pools under his head. His hands and legs are broken, his head is askew and his eyes are wide and staring, with an expression of stark fear frozen on his face.

Bingo races ahead, with Manish's shoe still stuck in his saddle. He disappears into the mist and the sound of the galloping horse slowly fades away. The silence is absolute again but this time, it is deafening.

***

Up at Sunrise Point, the sun comes out—a big ball of red and gold fire—and takes everyone's breath away. Aashu is mesmerised, and so is Rashid, though he has seen this sight almost every day of his life. It's God's riches to people like them who have no other, his grandmother used to say. Thinking of her makes him sad and he turns to look at his father who is looking at the path which has brought them up here. The young boy follows suit, his back turned to the glorious sunrise.

"Where is my father?" asks Avi, his face clouded with worry. Rahim is afraid that something bad has happened to sahab but by now, he knows to keep his mouth shut.

"Your hunches are *Allah ki den*. They are God's gifts to you, beta. But the world sees them as curses. So keep them to yourself." His mother's voice reaches out to him from beyond the grave; it is weak but wise.

He looks at the anxious boy and tells him gently, "Don't worry, baba. Your father must have gone to another Point. He will be here soon. Meanwhile, why don't you turn around and watch the sun go up?"

"It's so dark," Avi whispers, though the sunlight is bright now. Rahim understands the twelve-year-old boy's sense of dread. His nostrils twitch and he sniffs like his horses. He can smell death in the air.

3

The Malhotras Come to Matheran

Late, the next afternoon, a family of five disembarks at Dasturi Naka. Since Matheran promotes eco-tourism, no cars are allowed beyond this point. There is a parking lot for tourists where they can leave their vehicles and proceed ahead on foot.

A ten-minute walk brings them to Aman Lodge Station from where there is a mini train every half hour to Matheran which is no more than a fifteen-minute ride. For the more adventurous, there are horses. For the elderly and those who are not keen on riding or trekking, there are hand-pulled rickshaws waiting to lug them up the hill.

The Malhotras, however, don't look like the usual tourists. For one, they have brought along a pile of luggage, including items of furniture. The porters and cart-pullers at the Naka are delighted as they unload all the baggage, knowing that the family will need help to ferry their bags and boxes, and wonder how much fee to ask for without raising suspicions about overcharging.

Aditya and Kiara are in their thirties. She is a pretty woman with a cloud of dark hair that has escaped the hairband and is pooling around a face dominated by a pair of laughing hazel eyes. She is slim but fit from regular gymming. Lugging a heavy backpack, she is trying valiantly to keep their brat pack from racing around like headless chicken.

Aditya is around five feet ten inches—lithe but with the wide shoulders and strong legs of an athlete. He displays the shrewdness of a successful businessman as he haggles with the driver of the van which has brought them to Dasturi and now wants a little extra fare. "No way am I paying you even a rupee more; a deal is a deal," he tells the grumbling driver, insisting that if they don't part ways amicably, he will not call him for the return journey.

"Oh, so you will be going back to Mumbai? From all the luggage you brought along, I had assumed that you were moving here for good. How long will you be in Matheran?" the driver asks, instantly interested in another chance to earn some money.

Aditya shrugs. "At least a couple of days unless my wife and the kids fall in love with the place like I did and want to settle down here. I know I wouldn't mind. Mumbai is maddening with its crowds, and the pollution is killing us. But we will still need to get back to Mumbai to pick up the rest of our stuff."

"Where will you be staying?" the driver prods. Aditya's answer—"Cecil Lodge"—prompts him to raise his eyebrows, and without another word, he pockets the fare and drives off.

***

Kiara has been keeping an eye on the porter who rushed across to help unload their many suitcases and cartons of appliances and a few chairs and tables. She is also keeping a close watch over seven-year-old Siddharth, who is the most excitable of the three kids.

The porter is an adolescent of around sixteen, with the first fuzz of facial hair and a voice that is still to crack. While he stacks everything in neat piles, she asks him his name. "Gagan," he replies shyly and turns red because the beautiful memsahab has expressed a personal interest in him instead of looking through him like most tourists do.

To him, she looks like a movie star and with the innocence intrinsic in *pahadi log*, he asks her if she is one. Kiara bursts out laughing. "No, I am just a wife, mother and homemaker for now. The triple responsibilities leave me with time for little else. But one day, I want to become an interior decorator."

The boy doesn't understand what an interior decorator is but smiles back, saying, "You are as beautiful as Alia Bhatt… You remember *Student of the Year*'s Radha, don't you? She is my favourite actress. I have seen her *Badrinath Ki Dulhania* five times and I can dance to "Tamma Tamma" better than that Varun Dhawan. You are from Mumbai, have you met her?"

Kiara laughs harder. "No, I haven't. We don't move around in the same social circles unfortunately. Like you, I have only seen her on screen, though I prefer her as the spy in *Raazi*. I have seen that film twice."

Emboldened by the exchange, Gagan exclaims, "Oh, I love *Raazi*. I have seen it ten times! What's your name?"

"Kiara" makes him beam broadly. "Now I know why you look familiar—you resemble Kiara Advani! I have seen *Shershah* eight times already just for her. If I were Sidharth Malhotra… or rather Vikram Batra…I would have made sure I did not get shot in Kargil."

To his disappointment, this time, the memsahab does not react. She is distracted by the thirteen-year-old twins, Sara and

Sana, her nieces, who are excitedly pointing to the mini train chugging up the hills. Sid has seen it too and is impatiently tugging at her hand, wanting to run off in its direction. Kiara is trying desperately to retain her hold on the child, not wanting to get too far away from their belongings.

Where is Aditya? Why is he taking so long? She spots him at a distance, still negotiating with the cart-pullers. Tutting her annoyance, she looks around, her eyes drawn to the many OB vans stationed around the parking lot. There's a lot of hustle bustle around them, with TV anchors giving live updates on camera while a group of locals are crowded around a TV monitor.

She nods towards them and curiously asks, "Gagan, *kya ho raha hai wahan*? Why has Matheran suddenly become so happening? *Koi* film shooting *ho raha hai kya* or is there some politician here?"

The boy looks at her in surprise. "You don't know, memsahab?... About the accident?"

A bemused Kiara shakes her head, and Gagan brings her up to date on Manish Shah's tragic death even as a newsreader appears on the screen, saying, "Matheran Hindustan *ka ek hi aisa* hill station *hai jo apne* green zone *ke liye maana jaata hai.* This unique holiday destination in the state of Maharashtra is still pollution-free because no vehicles are allowed beyond this point, Dasturi Naka, except for hand-pulled rickshaws and carts. There are of course horses and one of them was responsible..."

A little way off, Gagan is telling Kiara about the sahab falling to his death from a horse the previous morning. She is shocked and asks, "How did it happen?"

"He was on his way to Sunrise Point with his two sons early in the morning. Some are saying Rahim chacha and Rashid bhai—they were the ghodawallahs accompanying them—are to blame for letting him ride Bingo alone," Gagan mutters, frowning darkly as he looks in the direction of the OB vans.

On the screen, a TV anchor is saying, "And not just the local horsemen who hand the reins over for a few hundred rupees, even irresponsible tourists are to blame for such accidents. Riding alone without helmets and pushing their horses to run at full speed on the treacherous trails without a thought for their own safety can be fatal..."

***

Back in Dune Barr House, Manish's widow, Chetna, whose face is puffed and streaked with tears, is speaking to the cops. "But, inspector, Manish was a skilled and experienced rider. He has…had…been riding since he was in school. He never had a problem controlling any horse. I'm pretty sure something or someone spooked the animal."

Her cellphone rings; it's her mother-in-law. "Yes, Baa, the post-mortem is finally done and they are expected to hand over the body in an hour. Aashu is at the hospital. As soon as he returns, we will be on our way."

She eyes the cops and adds, somewhat belligerently, "That is, if the policewallas leave us and stop asking the same questions over and over again. As if they are going to bring my husband back."

She breaks down, and Avi, suddenly looking very grown up, walks up to the cops and says, "Please leave my mother alone. She is the only one we have left now. If only we hadn't gone riding today…" His eyes flood too.

In the marketplace, near the police station, Rashid, who has finally been let off after being questioned for hours, is chatting with his friends. "I warned Sahab not to go towards Garbett

Point. That's why Bingo bolted. He is always skittish when he is there. We still haven't found him after the accident. Some are saying he fell into the ravines but Abba believes he's still alive and running scared. They found one of his horse shoes by the railway tracks."

His words leave the surrounding crowd murmuring among themselves. Both Garbett Point and the nearby railway tracks have been declared no-man's zone. No one ventures there anymore. The babu from the city was foolish to not heed Rashid's warning, think the locals. Now, thanks to him, there are presswallahs and policewallahs milling around their hill station. They dislike both as they keep the tourists away, which is bad for business.

***

Aditya has joined Kiara. Gagan is telling her that there is a *bhoot* on the railway tracks. "And what does this ghost look like? Is she as beautiful as my wife or ugly as sin?" Aditya asks with a twinkle in his eyes.

Realising that the man is laughing at him, Gagan clams up, mumbling that those who have seen the *bhoot* are no longer alive to tell the tale, including the *shehri* babu who died yesterday. This makes Aditya guffaw loudly. An on-ground TV journalist is reporting live: "Businessman Manish Shah passed away yesterday after he fell off his horse. He died from a brain haemorrhage. His life might have been saved had he got timely medical aid, *par unhe toh* first aid *bhi nahin mila*. By the time he was discovered and they got him to the local hospital, it was too late to save him."

On the TV screen, a debate is raging, with a local politician thundering, "With regards to Manish Shah's death, the government is responsible for not developing this heritage site properly. There are no lights in Matheran, no road signs. Hell, there are no roads to speak of!"

Aditya wrests his attention away from the chaos around him and focuses on the task at hand. His son is a bundle of excitable energy. He collars the boy and holds him tight. While Sid looks longingly at Matheran's famous toy train from a distance, his father vigilantly watches the porters load the furniture and boxes on their *thelas* while they cry "*dum laga ke haisha*" in unison. It's so easy to lose count of boxes and bags in the melee, and he doesn't want to misplace anything. He feels reassured to see that his wife too is counting under her breath.

Once everything is loaded to their satisfaction, the Malhotras set off. Sid is piggy-backing on his father's shoulders, while Kiara has linked arms with her nieces. Four porters are wheeling their carts as the group trudges towards Matheran.

4

Cecil Lodge

In half an hour, the Malhotras reach the hill station. As they draw closer to Matheran railway station, one of the porters says apprehensively, "We can't take the short cut over the railway tracks anymore, sahab. We will take the longer route to the lodge."

Aditya frowns and responds, "Why? I always took the short cut when I was here last."

"That must have been before Covid came calling?" enquires the porter. When Aditya nods, he adds, sighing, "A lot of things have changed since then. Now, that way is not safe."

Aditya nods again, not wanting to argue. It was quite a task getting these four to agree to ferry their luggage in the first place. As soon as he mentioned that he wanted to go to Cecil Lodge, many of the porters at Dasturi Naka melted away. He had to promise these four double the usual fare before they agreed to come along.

Sid is jigging about on his dad's shoulders. "Papa, are we going to Hogwarts? Can I become a wizard like Harry Potter and make you disappear by saying Abracadabra?"

Kiara bursts out laughing. "Woah, champ, slow down. We need your dad around."

Aditya is also chuckling. "Wait till we reach Cecil to become Potter, Siddie." He turns to his wife and exclaims, "I can't wait to show you all the place. I promise, you are all going to love it."

Kiara smiles at her husband and says, "Going by the pictures you showed us, I am sure we will."

A stray pup has joined them and is walking ahead, as if showing them the way. Sara nudges her twin and whispers, "What a cutie! Let's adopt him. I always wanted a dog but you know Mummy won't let us keep one in Mumbai. She says it will feel stifled in the apartment. But here, there is plenty of room for it to run around."

Sana, the quieter of the two who usually falls in with her sister, older by four minutes, asks, "What should we name him?"

Sara's response is immediate and prosaic. "He's brown... so, Brownie."

Sid, while talking nineteen to the dozen with his parents, has his ears tuned into their conversation as usual and butts in saying, "No, he's showing us the way. Let's call him Google."

Both girls agree that Google is an apt name for the pup whose stumpy tail hasn't stopped wagging. Kiara smiles up at her son. "Well done, Siddie!" The little boy beams proudly. She turns to the twins and says, "You can keep him if he stays but you have to give Google a bath. He surely hasn't had one in ages and he smells." She wrinkles her nose, and they promise to keep him clean.

They have reached the market now, and Aditya can see that the girls are tiring. Even he's finding it difficult to lug around Sid, who is no more as little as he once was. He decides that it would be prudent to hire three horses for the kids. It's still three kilometres to the lodge, which would take at least another half-hour or even longer, given their sluggish pace. He wants to get there before the sun goes down. The mountains can be treacherous in the dark, and he doesn't want to take any chances with an excitable child like Sid.

"Cecil Lodge *chalega*?" he asks and is surprised when one ghodawallah after another shakes his head, offering lame excuses. "*Nahin*, sahab, it's too far." "It is already late and by the time we return, it will be dark." "We will not get any return fare on the way back because no one lives around the lodge." And so on. The best one is reserved for last: "Cecil Lodge is haunted, sahab. It's been shut for a while now. *Koi nahi rehta wahan*. The place is empty except for her *bhoot*. Why do you want to go there? There are plenty of good hotels around here and we will take you to one."

Aditya throws his head back and laughs, saying, "Haunted, my foot! There are no ghosts in my lodge. Yes, it's mine now. I'm the new owner of Cecil Lodge. And I'm going to settle down there with my family."

The men exchange looks but don't react to his grandiose announcement. Deflated, Aditya repeats, "I need three horses for the kids. Are any of you willing to come along?"

The silence that follows is strained, broken by a ghodawallah who reiterates that the lodge is a long way off. "*Bahut door hai*," he mumbles.

Aditya is beginning to look irritated. He has been trying to call someone non-stop since they got off at Dasturi Naka but can't seem to get through. "Damn network!" he mutters.

Forcing a smile, he cajoles the horseman who just spoke up. "Boss, 600 *ke jagah* 900 *rupiya le lo par chalo ab*. No more excuses. I did say I would pay extra, and I am not the kind of person to go back on my word. I can understand that you are reluctant because you will not get any return fares, but I will make it worth your time and effort."

The men are unmoved by the bribe, which is surprising because usually money can buy you anything in Matheran. But in this case, they are rooted to the spot. At his wit's end, Aditya tries once again to put through a call and fails. Exasperated, he asks if anyone knows Suresh ghodawallah.

Rashid, who has been standing by silently and listening to the exchange, pipes up, "Who doesn't know that *bewda*!"

Aditya is startled. When did Suresh start drinking? They had met just before the pandemic brought travel to a standstill for over a year and a half. At the time, he had seemed like a *chai-paani* kind of guy—friendly and sunny-tempered.

Realising that the elders are angry with him for running down one of their own, Rashid tries to cover up his gaffe, muttering that Suresh chacha only drinks at night.

"And since when did he start drinking?" Aditya asks. This time, one of the older men answers him. "Since his stable caught fire. He lost four horses. He's been depressed ever since."

Mumbling almost to himself, Rashid says, "We've lost a horse too. Abbu has been out of his mind wondering where Bingo has disappeared. I hope he won't turn into a *bewda* too." Even if anyone hears him, they don't react.

Aditya asks if anyone can call Suresh for him, and the elderly ghodawallah immediately dispatches Rashid to get him. The boy goes running down the hill in the direction of the stables. "He should be here in ten minutes," says the horseman to assure Aditya, who strolls across to a nearby stall for some bottled water and ice candies for the kids. They are beginning to look hot, and he knows from experience that Sid can be more than a handful when he is tired.

He returns to where the ghodawallahs are still standing—a silent lot, they are not interested in making conversation after learning that he has bought Cecil Lodge. Aditya muses over their strange behaviour, tapping his feet impatiently as he waits for Suresh.

The horseman, who is in his late fifties and looks somewhat dishevelled but excited, comes hurrying along and embraces Aditya warmly. "Baba, *kaisa hai tu? Bahut din baad yahan aaya hai*, but now you have come with your family." He smiles at Kiara and doffs his cap in a respectful greeting.

Aditya looks relieved that the horseman still remembers him, though he can smell the alcohol on his breath. He asks—somewhat tentatively, given the earlier spate of refusals from other horsemen—if he can drop the kids off on his horses. Suresh agrees immediately, though there comes up the slightest hesitation when he learns that their destination is Cecil Lodge, something only one as sensitive to vibes as Aditya picks up on. The kids whoop in delight and even Kiara looks relieved. Thankfully, Suresh doesn't change his mind and goes off to get his horses.

***

As they trudge through the woods and up the muddy trail, with Google in front of them, Aditya asks Suresh why the other ghodawallahs were so reluctant to accompany them. The horseman's laugh is forced. "Union politics, baba. They are giving Matheran a bad name. But don't worry. If you need anything...*koi bhi kaam ho*...just call me. Bhabhi-ji *ko bhi mera* number *de dena*. I am at your service at all times of the day." Kiara smiles her thanks at the burly, unshaven man, who reeks of cheap booze. Right now, he is their saviour. Aditya forwards Suresh's phone number to her. She would like to ask him some questions about the lodge that no one wants to visit, but her husband's warning look stops her. She is surprised—Aditya is normally a friendly and talkative guy and Suresh seems to be one too—but stays silent.

After a while, Suresh asks Aditya why he invested in a property in Matheran. "That's the business I run, Suresh bhai. I buy properties which are auctioned by banks, caught in legal hassles, have unpaid mortgages or require distress sales. I buy them for a throwaway price and renovate and refurbish these properties to either put them back in the market or up on AirBnb," explains Aditya.

Suresh is impressed and muses to himself that Aditya's marketing skills must bring in huge profits. Encouraged by his genuine delight, Aditya tells him that he always dreamt of having a vacation home in Matheran. "While Cecil Lodge is being renovated, the five of us will be staying on the campus in the villa just behind it. The kids are still being schooled online and Kiara can help me oversee the interiors. I don't know if we can settle there, what with school and work, but we definitely want to visit frequently," he explains. "Network *ka* problem *hoga*. Near the lodge, within a radius of two kilometres, there's no mobile tower, so you might have a problem getting through," he warns.

Dismayed, Aditya points out that during his last visit when he finalised the deal, there was talk of two new towers being installed. Suresh admits that they were installed but explains that monkeys and rains brought them down.

"No wonder I haven't been able to get through to you since we arrived!" Aditya exclaims and Suresh reminds him that since they are high up in the mountains, they will have to get used to such connectivity problems.

Kiara's smile has turned into a sulk as it dawns on her that they could be cut off from family and friends. "Why did you buy a property here? Who would want to stay in this place if they are unable to communicate with anyone?" she snaps, her temper flaring.

Aditya's nerves are frayed too after the long trip, and he argues a trifle heatedly that those who are looking for an AirBnb want to be close to nature and disconnected from civilization. "They want to detox. Refresh and rejuvenate. They are not looking to stay in touch. They are looking for a clean and hygienic place, simple and wholesome food and peace and quiet," he says to her in a sharp tone, making Sid look at him. His dad rarely gets angry.

Kiara stomps off alone, with Google at her heels. She is bugged that she may not be able to have her daily confabs with her sister, Sonal, Sara and Sana's mother. Only a couple of years separate the siblings, and they are as thick as Sonal's twins. Kiara had promised Sonal daily updates from Matheran and plenty of selfies, but now that may not be possible.

She just hopes the girls' schooling is not interrupted or her sister will kill her. Thank God there is still a week to go before their Diwali vacation ends. By then, she hopes, Aditya will have the wifi going. Else, he will have to take them back, and then it will get even more lonely.

Suresh ponders over Aditya's words. "You are right. Some people, particularly the goras, want to come to places like this for shanti and simple living. They want to be away from all the noise and stress of the city. Don't worry, baba. Once bhabhi-ji sees Cecil, she will not have any complaints. Aditya baba *ka* choice always A-grade," he booms.

Touched, Aditya gently punches him on the back, and they walk together companionably till Sara, whose horse is trotting alongside, asks petulantly, "Uncle, *aur kitna duur*?"

Suresh tells her that they are almost there, and she pouts while pointing out that he has been saying this for the last fifteen minutes. He laughingly tells her that because Cecil is the last destination in Matheran, it's a long way off. "Once you get to the lodge, if you look straight ahead over the valley, you might be able to see your home in Mumbai," he promises. The kids are instantly excited and strain their eyes.

Kiara has returned to the group, grumbling that there are no hotels nearby. The market and railway station are also far away, and even the ghodawallahs are reluctant to come out to the lodge. Aditya tells her in a softer, more placating tone that they will learn to enjoy the peace and privacy the lodge offers them.

"And if you need to go anywhere, we can always call Suresh bhai, right?" he says and turns to smile at the ghodawallah, who nods but doesn't smile back.

A minute later, they all reach the gates of Cecil Lodge. The ghodawallah quickly lifts the kids down from their horses and asks permission to leave, saying that the sun will go down soon and that it's a long way to his home.

Aditya nods and gives him a large tip. A smile again lights up Suresh's swarthy face as he counts the notes, realising he has got double the usual fare. "Tomorrow morning, do you want me to take the kids up to Sunrise Point?" he asks eagerly and a clamour of 'yes' goes up. He promises to be back with the horses by 5 a.m. and, after a round of goodbyes, leaves.

***

Aditya unlatches the white latticed gate. It swings open with a screech.

"Oooo, just like in those ghost stories," Sara observes and her uncle responds laughingly, "No, just needs some oiling and..."

He stops abruptly as a pack of dogs races wildly towards them from inside the compound, barking frenziedly. Kiara freezes and the kids run behind her, throwing their arms around her legs and rendering her immobile in the process.

Surprisingly, Google distracts the attention of the dogs, barking and running down the road and into the bushes up ahead. They chase after the pup. Aditya and Kiara hurry the kids through the gate and latch it securely behind them. They are safe but a loud howl, followed by frenzied barking, makes them afraid for the puppy.

Fortunately, the children's attention has been diverted by swings and a seesaw, which are all in working condition. There's also a badminton court, though overrun with weeds, and a merry-go-round.

Kiara's eyes are on the boutique hotel in front of her. It is larger than she had expected, with a certain old-world charm. Steps painted a cheery red lead up to a wide porch with red trimming. There are rooms all around it. The doors and windows are white, like the walls, and look freshly painted even though the lodge has been vacant. Aditya must have spruced up the place for them, she thinks. Her earlier annoyance forgotten, Kiara turns to smile at him.

The kids, who have been running around the well-built but worn-out playground, enter the lodge. As they patter down a long corridor, with Aditya and Kiara following them, the children check out the many rooms on either side. They are big and spartan but clean—the beds are spread with freshly laundered sheets; the fans hanging from the high ceilings are turning slowly; the windows are open, bringing in the cool mountain air and leading the windchimes to tinkle.

Kiara notices that the attached baths are in pretty good shape too except for a few damp patches on the walls due to monsoon rains and some broken tiles. "It's well maintained," she congratulates her husband, who admits that he needs to thank the caretaker for taking such good care of the property.

"Shivaji is a nice guy and very helpful. I wonder where he is. He knew we were coming today," Aditya says before offering to show the others the villa where they will be staying and wandering back towards the front door. They follow him out. The one-storey villa is at the farthest end of the property and overlooks the valley. It's painted in the same white and red colours of the lodge and encircled by an enclosed verandah, which has a small gate. Kiara is the first to walk up the pathway towards it. As she unlatches the gate, she is startled to see Google sitting on the verandah and wagging his tail.

"I thought you were dead. How did you get away from those dogs and come here? We had locked the gates. I guess, there's a way from the back," she whispers as she bends down to pat the mutt. "Sara...Sana...Sid...Look, who's here," she shouts over her shoulder.

Seeing Google, everyone's mood lifts. Aditya brings out a bowl of water for the puppy, who laps it up thirstily. He notices a couple of dogs growling at them from behind the bushes in the garden. He looks around, bends down, picks up some stones and aims straight at them.

Yelping, they run off, with Google seemingly pleased at their discomfort. Aditya makes a mental note to fence the property's backside at the earliest to keep the hounds at bay. He has been to see the lodge just once before today, on a short visit. The deal was setted through Zoom calls because of Covid restrictions. Maybe he should have waited and not been in such a hurry, but it was such a steal that he couldn't refrain from closing the deal in a rush.

***

The porters are bringing in the luggage, and soon everyone gets busy putting away the bags, boxes and furniture. Once they have unloaded everything, Aditya sees them to the gate, making sure to tip them generously. They go away happy, but he notices that they don't offer to come over again—this is surprising.

As he turns, he is startled to find a short, stocky man staring at him. He is ugly as sin, with flies buzzing around him. He puts down the two steel buckets he is carrying. "*Paani*. I went out to the woods to get water," he says in a hoarse voice, pointing to them.

It takes a few seconds to place him, but Aditya finally remembers the broker mentioning that Shivaji had a cousin, Madhu, staying with him, a handyman of sorts. When he asks if he is Madhu, the man nods and says in strong Marathi-accented Hindi that he has made *khichdi, kadhi aur sabzi* and left the food in the dining room of the lodge. He has also cleaned both the lodge and the villa. "*Jevan thevla aahe, sab saaf kar diya hai*," he mutters, looking to Aditya's left.

Trying to lock eyes with him, Aditya realises he is cock-eyed. He asks about Shivaji, the caretaker, and Madhu doesn't reply. With his eyes darting, he states that he has to leave now. "Before *she* comes..."

Before Aditya can enquire about 'she', Kiara and the kids shout out to him excitedly from the verandah of the bungalow. Madhu looks in their direction and then walks away towards the main gate, leaving the buckets where he had placed them. Aditya wonders if he should call him back but decides against it. The guy seems weird, but he has done all the work and it is getting dark. He will talk to Shivaji tomorrow, decides Aditya.

Grimacing, he picks up the heavy buckets and walks back towards the villa.

The signboard over Cecil Lodge flickers. Madhu stares up at it for a long moment and then hurries down the road, grousing, "Stupid city folks! Why did they have to come here?"

5

Evil Dead

Suresh is sitting in the stable looking desolately at the still-empty horse stalls, remembering Sam, Basanti, Zohra and Bahadur, who had perished in a fire a couple of years ago. His heart bleeds when he thinks of the horses. He can still hear their panicked whinnies as the fire raged around them. He had tried so hard but could not save them.

In his nightmares, he can still see the flames rushing towards them. And he can see *her*. All the alcohol in the world has not been able to give him even one night of peaceful sleep.

He looks around, a dazed expression on his face. The stable is still singed in places, he notes in the light of the lone bulb dangling from the middle. Perhaps sensing his distress, the half-a-dozen horses around him make their presence felt, some stamping their feet, while others snort and neigh. Suresh breathes in their familiar smell and is soothed.

Pouring himself a drink from the quarter bottle he carries around in his pocket these days, the ghodawallah smiles at them. He lifts the glass to his lips, hoping it will numb the excruciating pain in his gut and wipe away the dark memories.

His wife, Suman, is cooking dinner in the shack adjourning the stables. They have just had another fight. As soon as he returned home after dropping Aditya baba and his family, she confronted him, asking if he had been paid for the job.

He marvels at her network. Even though Suman rarely leaves the house these days, she knows exactly where he has been all day and what he has been doing. He wonders at her sources. Must be the young boys who are always dropping by "to meet chachi." Bloody spies all of them, passing on information to her for a few laddoos and *chikkis*. When he chases after them, they run off, chortling, "Bewda! Bewda!"

His drinking is becoming a problem, he knows, not just within the community but also with his wife. "*Paisa laya ya phir daaru mein sab uda ke aaya*? These days you spend everything you earn on cheap liquor," Suman had said sniffing disgustedly earlier in the evening as the stench from his person had hit her.

Throwing up his hands in frustration, Suresh had exclaimed, "What do you think! Baba is an old customer—he not only paid me but even gave me extra. And he has called me tomorrow to take the children to Sunrise Point. With him around, we won't have to worry about money for sometime. He is a good guy and we get along well."

Digging into his pocket, he had taken out a few soiled notes and almost thrown them at her. "Here, take your money. That's all that makes you happy these days. *Ab much much mat kar*. Let me sit in peace for sometime in the stable with my children."

She had flounced off in the direction of the kitchen, grumbling that all the money he earned was either spent on his booze or feed for the horses. "Only after that *hum logon ka* number *lagne ka*. One of these days, both you and I will die—*tu peete peete, main pakate pakate*," she had shouted. Suresh had mumbled, "How I wish I could die and join my horses in heaven!" She had shot back that he would probably go to hell. "With *her*," she had added.

Just before Suman could bang the stable door shut, he had shouted back, determined to have the last word. "After I am gone, you will realise my worth. Our boys are gone. Off to Mumbai. They are not coming back. And the few friends we have here are not going to stay around and listen to your *bak bak*."

She used to be a sweet, smiling woman, Suresh now recalls. But in the last two years, she has changed. Since…he swallows hard, reining in his thoughts. No, he is not going to let them wander in that direction again. He lifts the glass and takes a big gulp, the alcohol searing his insides. Suman was right, he acknowledges—one of these days, he is going to topple over and die. He just hopes it is the alcohol that kills him. And not *her*.

Half an hour later, Suman walks into the stable, wielding a ladle. She is quieter. His parting words have hit home. Despite everything, she still loves Suresh. If only she had taken up that job at the lodge, he begins to think…

"Dinner is ready," she mutters. "I've made *surmai*, your favourite fish. You better hurry. It won't taste as good if you let it grow cold."

He puts down his drink wordlessly and lumbers after her. They are almost at the door of the stable when Suman casually asks, "Where are these people you dropped off staying? Usha Escort? Or Byke Hotel?"

Suresh waits a beat before softly saying, "Cecil…Cecil Lodge!"

The ladle Suman is carrying drops to the ground with a clatter. She freezes and then eventually turns to look at her husband. "You went there again? You went to Cecil?"

His face is blank, expressionless. There is a shared secret in their eyes, which none of them voices. Without exchanging another word, the couple head home, but dinner has lost its appeal.

***

Around the same time, an Innova drives into Dasturi Naka. It's dark by now, and the two men who alight are met by a third holding a torch to light the way. He escorts them across the parking lot to the Matheran Entry Office. There they are introduced to the officer on duty, Amit Kotkar. "Inspector Yogesh Todkar and his assistant, Constable Amole Tembe, from Mumbai Crime Branch. They have come to investigate the accidental death of Manish Shah," Kotkar is told.

He stands up respectfully and offers the inspector a chair, hollering, "*Arre chai-paani lao* sahab *ke liye*. Sir, why don't you take a seat."

Todkar remains standing, curtly rapping out, "*Rehne ka bandobast kahan kiya*? Where are we putting up?"

Before Kotkar can reply, Tembe tells him to give them a good, clean lodge because the inspector suffers from a dust allergy. "*Waise* the weather is good, but make sure our rooms are air-conditioned. *Par* room heater *bhi hona mangta*, and quilts too, in case it gets cold at night. *Aur haan ek baat bahut* important, the food must be excellent. Mutton, chicken, surmai fry. Sahab is a non-vegetarian and so am I. So no *ghas phus*," he informs, lowering his voice to a whisper so that his demands are not heard by the guy who brought them here.

Kotkar assures him that they will be taken good care of and calls for a hand-pulled rickshaw to take them to Diwadkar Hotel. "Hotel first class *hai*. Right in front of the station so commuting will not be a problem. You will get horses and rickshaws easily," he informs before whispering that the hotel also has an alcohol permit, so they can relax in the bar after their long journey to Matheran.

For the first time since they have arrived, the inspector cracks a smile and ushers Tembe out, saying, "*Kal sakali kaam shuru karuya, aaj araam.*" A few minutes later, they are escorted out to where the rickshaw is waiting.

Kotkar keeps his cool till they are out of earshot. He then explodes, "*Saale harami, muft ka chandan, ghis mere nandan.* I know what will go into their report, and it definitely won't be what happens at the hotel tonight. Mutton, chicken, surmai fry. Rascals in uniform, using an accident to get a free vacation!"

***

In the villa where they are staying, Sid has found a treasure trove in a small storeroom on the first floor. It is filled with discarded stuff. He has dug out a tricycle handle from one of the boxes and runs down the stairs with it, ringing the bell still attached to it. Tring! Tring! In the living room, he walks into Sara and Sana's Tik Tok video. Their screams bring Kiara down the stairs from the master bedroom as she wonders why all hell has broken loose. While reprimanding Sid for making a nuisance of himself, Kiara notes that some of the existing pieces of furniture in the living room are expensive antiques. It is obvious that the previous owners were well off, and she wonders why they left the pieces behind when they could have easily sold them to one of the lodges around.

A rocking chair by the window catches her attention. It's the perfect place to sit with Sid at the end of a busy day and rock him to sleep. She had always wanted a chair exactly like this one. It is obvious that it is old, its upholstery having faded in places with time, but she already loves it.

She looks towards the small kitchen adjoining the living room and suddenly realises that she is famished, which is not surprising given that they have not eaten anything since they grabbed a sandwich on the way. What is rather surprising is that the kids haven't mentioned food even once. Being in a new place has kept hunger at bay, but soon they will be asking for food.

She walks into the kitchen: it is bare except for a few plates and mugs. She is dismayed and begins hoping that Aditya has made some arrangements for dinner. Had they been in Mumbai, she would have placed an order, but she is pretty certain Swiggy doesn't deliver pizzas and biryani to Cecil. All they have left are a few packets of biscuits and some energy bars, which won't suffice.

Sana is playing her Yamaha synthesiser, filling the house with music. Sara has wandered off to the window, looking out at the unkempt garden. She's quiet and perhaps a wee bit homesick for her mummy and daddy.

Sid has wandered out into the yard and is running around in circles, the cycle handle still in his hand. Along with the bell, there's a rearview mirror attached to it. He keeps looking into it, laughing and chatting with an imaginary someone. Kiara smiles as she looks at him from the window. "He always did have an imagination!" she tells Sara.

Sara doesn't reply but laughs out loud when with a loud thumping sound, a number of monkeys jump on the roof, scaring away Sid as he scurries back in. She turns away from the window to tease the little boy for being a "scaredy cat".

Minutes later, it's quiet again, but a strange energy is hovering around the campus. The merry-go-round outside the lodge suddenly starts with a squeak and slowly moves around in circles. No one notices except for the monkeys, which screech and disappear into the woods.

The seesaw goes up and down and the swings move on their own. Google barks from the porch. The dog keeps wandering off around the property but always returns.

The faint figure of a woman is walking down the road towards Cecil Lodge, humming softly. She is there and yet not there. She reaches the gate. The road is quiet and empty until suddenly, one hears the clip clop of an approaching horse. She smiles.

In the flickering light of the lodge's signboard, a black horse suddenly appears out of the dark night. It is Bingo. His eyes are bloodshot, and he is foaming at the mouth. The horse looks at her and disappears around the bend, in the direction of the lake. The woman slips in through the gates.

***

Charlotte Lake, also known as Sharlott Lake, is a must-visit for tourists. The Pisharnath Temple on its left bank draws devotees, while Echo Point and Louisa Point to the right bring crowds of boisterous picnickers, along with solitary bird watchers.

Since the lake is the main source of filtered drinking water in Matheran, swimming and boating are strictly forbidden. But the placid waters, with the little waterfall close by, are popular selfie spots. The place is buzzing from sunrise to sunset, but after that it is deserted.

Tonight, mist, like a whiff of smoke, rises from the lake. Its waters are shimmering in the light of the full moon. In the woods, a snake slithers through the fallen leaves, disturbed from its resting place by the sound of approaching footsteps.

An *aghori* baba, his bare chest and face smeared with ashes, walks into view. Another man, a dark shadow, follows in his footsteps. The two continue walking till they reach a clearing deep in the forest. The ground has been swept clean. In the centre, some rocks have been arranged in a circle, twigs and dry leaves stacked in the middle to build a fire.

The man accompanying baba takes out two mats from the large cloth bag he is carrying and lays them out on opposite sides. Baba sits on one, cross-legged, and with one strike of the match, he lights the fire. His companion sits down across from the godman, who has started chanting, even as the flames flicker and slowly grow into a robust blaze.

The darkness is now lit by the full moon and the fire. Baba flicks open the mouth of the sack he has set next to him. From inside it, he pulls out a bleating kid. From a plantain leaf near the fire, he scoops up a handful of *gulal* and smears the white goat with the red colour. The animal is restless, trying to escape his confining hands, perhaps sensing danger, but is caught in a death grip.

The chanting grows louder and more frenzied. Then in a flash of blurred movement, the baba slashes the goat's neck with a knife. As fresh blood gushes out, some of it spraying over him, he wrenches off the animal's head. Lifting the body of the still-twitching animal, he pours the blood into a human skull and drinks from it deeply. Once the skull is empty, he places it back on the ground, wipes his mouth, leaving behind a streak of blood, and starts chanting again.

When the chanting reaches a crescendo, he digs into his sack again. As the other man flinches, instinctively knowing there are more deaths in store, baba draws out two small cages. One has a mouse scampering inside it and the other a fluttering chicken, both desperate to escape their confines.

Baba is now in a trance, his head bobbing wildly and his eyes wide open and crazed. One by one, the mouse and chicken are ritualistically slaughtered. His chants reverberate around the forest. After the sacrifices, baba's voice grows softer and his movements slow down. He finally falls silent just as the moon emerges from behind the dark clouds. In its light, one can see baba's face. He is a stranger. But the man sitting opposite him is Madhu, whose face is awash with sweat that mixes with the ashes and flows down in rivulets.

For the first time, Madhu speaks. "There are people in the lodge."

Baba shakes his head, saying, "They shouldn't be there. Send them away."

Madhu's lips twist. "The man has bought the place." He looks at the slaughtered corpses of the animals, blood streaming around them, and shudders as he says, "God alone knows why!"

The moon, perhaps disturbed by the devastation brought by death, disappears behind the clouds again. Cloaked in the darkness, baba packs up the remains of the rites, while Madhu washes out the clearing. Then, the two head back to the so-called civilised world.

***

Far away, a horse neighs. Rahim chacha, who is sitting with the bottle again, starts. Whose horse is that? Could it be his Bingo? Everyone around believes his baby is dead, but he refuses to give up hope. One day, Bingo will return to him. Or will he? He picks up the bottle.

Rashid looks at him unhappily from the corner. He has heard the horse too. He has been hearing it the last couple of nights. He knows that his abbu believes that it is Bingo. Perhaps he is right, but this horse sounds like an animal possessed.

6

Guests Who Came for Dinner

At the bungalow, the clock strikes nine. The kids, tired out by the excitement of the day, are running out of steam and nodding off. With a smile, Aditya picks up Sid from the rocking chair, which he seems to have turned into his nestling place. Even Kiara has a soft spot for this chair—it does look nice and comfortable, though it will have to be reupholstered, she thinks. Upon being lifted, his son grumbles sleepily, and the chair continues to rock, as if in protest against its guest being snatched away. Aditya laughs softly and, holding Sid in one arm, offers the other hand to the twins, pulling them up from the couch where they are sprawled out. "Come along, *bachcha* party. It's dinner time," he says.

He hands them their hoodies and makes a mental note to ask Shivaji to get a heater for the living room, given that they will be spending their evenings here and that winter is almost upon them. He will also have to see how best he can warm up the rest of the rather chilly rooms, in particular the bedrooms upstairs. They can always pull out the quilts they have brought along, and then again, he also has Kiara to make his blood steam and his senses reel, Aditya says to himself in reassurance.

Carrying Sid, he yells out to his wife. She has been arranging the bedrooms while he has been trying to set up the living room as best as he can. Kiara comes skipping down the stairs and asks him worriedly if there is any food for them. "All taken care of, my lady. You just need to follow your master to the lodge. We are having dinner *eshtyle mein*," he chortles, handing her a shawl and pulling on his sweater as he steps out of the bungalow with Sid still in his arms and Kiara following with the girls.

"Papa, where are we going?" whispers Sid, shivering as the cold seeps in through his thick hoodie. "Beta, there is a nice dining hall in the lodge just 500 metres away," Aditya replies, hurrying towards it.

Unfortunately, the lodge is equally draughty. As they walk down the dimly lit corridor, he notices with annoyance that not just the doors but also the windows of many of the bedrooms are open and curses Madhu for being so lax. The man had been in such a hurry to leave that he had not bothered to lock up behind him. It was like he was fleeing from the devil or rather the *bhoot* that has taken root in the minds of the locals.

Kiara folds her arms and clutches her shawl tightly, wishing she had worn a sweater too. She had imagined a lovely, chandelier-lit dinner, but this is no fun. She decides that from the next day, they will have their dinner at the villa itself. The kitchenette there is small but serviceable—good enough to heat up food and even stir up some soup and pasta.

As she hurries down the winding corridor, she notices that the beds have now been stripped bare. The rest of the furniture are dark shapes, giving the rooms an ominous air. Strangely, the door to one of the rooms—room no. 19—is shut.

Sensitive Sana voices her thoughts. "These rooms look really scary now. I wouldn't want to be living here." Sara, the practical one, points out that she will change her mind once the lodge is full of light and guests. Her twin shakes her head and asserts, "No, I won't. This place gives me the creeps."

Sid, who is clinging to his father's neck like a monkey, suddenly spots a carrom board, a table tennis table and a foosball table in the smoker's lounge, which is right outside the dining-room door. Enchanted, he leans down towards the foosball table, almost disbalancing his father.

Aditya tells him sharply that he can play with the dolls the next morning, for it's now time to get some food into his little stomach that is making funny, growling sounds. He tickles Sid in the tummy, and they enter the dining room laughing. Kaira and the twins are right behind them. Suddenly, all five stop short, their eyes and mouths wide open in amazement as they look up at large portraits adorning one of the walls.

With their backs to it, they don't see themselves reflected in the antique mirror behind them. A moment later, the faint silhouette of a woman materialises out of thin air as she watches them intently. Surprisingly, her image is not reflected in the looking glass, which is suddenly opaque now. Soon, the figure dissolves as though she never existed.

A hand reaches out and cranks the handle of the foosball table and the miniature players come alive, kicking the ball around. Sid would have clapped his hand in delight had he seen them, but his attention is elsewhere.

The dining room overlooks the badminton court. It is surrounded by spotlights, but they are doused. From the far end of the court, a boy of Sid's age watches the family inside. They are mutely gazing up at the photographs that stare down at them from the walls.

"Who's that?" Sara points to an elderly bearded man, whose gold-rimmed glasses are slipping down his long, pointed nose, with his disapproval apparent even in freeze-frame.

Sana squints and reads the name written in gold lettering on the dark frame. "Navroz Behram Edul Faram," she pronounces the words carefully. They are a mouthful.

Her eyes move to the next picture of an even more formidable gentleman. He is wearing traditional Parsi headdress and attire as he stands by a chair with a beautifully carved backrest, one hand resting on it and the other clutching a rolled-up umbrella. She reads out his name in a hushed tone. "And this is Faroukh…Faroukh Dinyar Irani."

"They are all old, with funny-sounding names," her twin announces, tossing her hair back disdainfully. Kiara swallows a laugh, not wanting to be disrespectful, but admits to herself that all these dour men and women, dreary in stark black and white, are indeed old. Well, not all, she corrects herself as she spots some younger faces, but none of them look like they are having much fun.

From his vantage position on his dad's shoulder, Sid points to a grand dame wearing an embroidered sari. Her blouse is trimmed with lace at the neck and around the sleeves and her face is bony and aristocratic, with pursed lips. Sana reads out her name painstakingly. "Fanibanda Rosy Pasta…Pastakia."

To everyone's surprise, Sid suddenly pipes up, "I don't like Fani. She was the one who made the others stay away. Look at her nose, just like Pinocchio." This time, Kiara can't smother her amusement and all five burst out laughing despite Fanibanda looking down at them disapprovingly.

Emboldened, the little boy looks at the picture of a mother with her newborn baby and, pointing to the infant, reports that this is Parzaan Dastoor Irani. His voice is assured and confident.

Sara peers at the picture and tells everyone that Sid just made that up because no names are written below this portrait. Laughing at his son's vivid imagination, Aditya turns towards the dining table, which is beautifully laid out with old-world china and silver cutlery. He notices Kiara's approving smile and thanks his stars that Madhu had bothered with some social graces even if his work wasn't quite up to the mark. The wife is finicky about such things, but she will certainly be disappointed with the meal, feels Aditya.

Seating Sid down on a chair and pulling one out for himself, Aditya removes the lid from a server apprehensively and breathes in the aroma of freshly cooked, steaming *dhanshak*. He bends and looks at the wax candles below the servers. So that's why the food is hot, he mumbles and feels rather warmly towards Madhu.

When he looks back at the meal, a frown forms between his brows. Didn't the helper say that he had made khichdi and kadhi for dinner? But here there's dhanshak, *pilaf* with peas and carrots. And *lagan nu* custard and a baked caramel pudding, which has caused the children to dance with delight.

Dinner is over in a jiffy as everyone is famished and the Parsi dishes are much appreciated. As she scrapes the last of the dessert from her plate, Kiara says, "You must introduce me to our excellent chef, Aditya. I want to learn how to make this custard."

He doesn't reply, wondering how Madhu, who looks and speaks like a *pucca* Maharashtrian, learnt how to make such exquisite cuisine and serve it with so much care. The man is a mystery.

***

Sid jumps out of his chair, which is a little too high for his short legs, and scurries to the washbasin at a far corner of the room. Across it is the large kitchen, which is covered in shadows. In the dustbin, Madhu's unappetizing khichdi and kadhi have been dumped. No one notices.

The little boy quickly rinses out his mouth and starts as he notices a dhanshak stain on his hoodie. He hopes his mother will not spot it. Sara and Sana are still at the table, cracking jokes about the Parsis in the photographs above. He turns back to the basin and almost screams out loud as a boy of his age stares back at him from the shadows of the kitchen. He's the same boy who has been watching them from the badminton court. With a finger on his lips, the boy cautions Sid to stay silent. He nods, instinctively understanding that his new buddy—Parzaan—doesn't want to befriend the rest of his family.

A sudden movement to his left makes him look in the direction. A spider is crawling up the wall. It is big, hairy and black, with beady eyes and eight spindly legs. This time he screams.

Kiara immediately rushes towards him, asking him what is wrong. He turns to look at her and then back to where the boy was standing. Parzaan is gone, but Sid's mother is by his side, asking him what frightened him. With a trembling finger he points to the wall. She raises her eyebrow and asks, "What?" The spider has disappeared too.

Something nudges Sid's leg. He looks down to see Google staring up at him from the kitchen, sitting at the exact spot where Parzaan had been standing. The puppy's eyes are bright, with his pink tongue hanging out. Sid points to him with a delighted smile. "Google is back."

Kiara is surprised to see the pup. How did the dog enter the lodge? She assumes that there is a back door in the kitchen.

Soon, everyone gathers around Google, wondering where he had disappeared.

Finally, Aditya breaks up the party, telling them it's time for bed. "Else you won't be able to go to Sunrise Point with Suresh uncle and the horses tomorrow morning. He did say he would be here at 5 a.m.," he reminds them. Instantly, the rebellion which was rising is quelled.

As Sana is walking out, she asks, "Masa, are Parsis Indians or foreigners? These people in the pictures look so different, especially the older ones. Nothing like Dadi and Dadu back home or even Nana and Nani in Delhi."

Aditya informs her that Parsis were originally Farsis from Persia, who fled to India to escape Muslim invaders centuries ago. "They sailed into Gujarat and never went back," he tells her.

"Oh, that's why they speak Gujarati with a funny accent… My Parsi friend in school taught me a lullaby her dadi used to sing to her. *Ah ha mari Dolly tu, kavi mari Dolly tu, aapu tu-ne badhdha jee, raku pet-ma chapi, Dolly mari motti thai, motti thai nasal-e jai…*" Listening to Sana, everyone laughs.

Not to be outshone by her twin, Sara informs that she has read that Parsis are a small community, which is decreasing in size every year. As Aditya nods in agreement, she wonders curiously if all the people whose pictures are up in the dining room are dead. Kiara tries to change the subject, telling the girl that her uncle is not Google.

Sara, who has been scrolling on her phone, pipes up, saying that Parsis are not Hindus, Muslims or Christians; they are Zoroastrians. She reads aloud, "And when they die, they are not burnt or buried. Instead, their bodies are left in the Tower of Silence for vultures to feast on…Ewww. Is that true, Uncle?"

Marvelling at the morbid curiosity of kids, Aditya tells her lightly that they will make a documentary on Parsis another day. They have reached the villa and he points to the upstairs bedroom. "It's goodnight and sweet dreams for now," he says firmly. The clock in the living room strikes ten. The villa is full of strange energies.

7

The Parsi Connection

In Diwadkar Hotel, the two cops are sitting at the bar nursing their whiskeys. Drunkenly, Inspector Todkar tells Tembe that he had come to Matheran with the missus *"shaadi ke paile"*. His assistant corrects him, pointing out that since he and Shanti-ji are married now, he should address her as *"baiko"*, and laughs that the English "missus" sounds like he is romancing someone else's wife.

Todkar is too wasted to get the PJ. Raising his glass to his lips, he slurs, "*Arre,* I am talking about Shanti *re.* Before our *lagna,* there was so much peace when I was around her. Now life *mein bas ashanti hi ashanti.* Bloody hell!"

Tembe, emboldened by the liquor, nudges him, saying, "*Dekho, sahib, idhar bhi shanti hai.*" Todkar starts and tries to hide his glass behind his back, apprehensively asking, "Shanti? Where is she?"

Tembe rolls his eyes and tells him that he was referring to the peace and quiet of Matheran. This time, his boss laughs immediately. "*Chaa maaila,* you scared me, *aai shapath.*" His subordinate pokes him in the ribs, retorting in an over-familiar tone, "*Baap, fattu hai re tu.*"

Tembe has definitely crossed the line, and despite his benign mood, Todkar reacts to the slight, reminding him that he is still his boss. Tembe jumps to his superior's feet immediately and salutes him.

Mollified, the inspector admits that while he is the boss at work, at home, his wife wears the pants. Wagging a finger at him, Todkar warns Tembe that once he is married, he will realise exactly what he means.

His assistant looks bemused, not understanding his meaning. Todkar asks, "*Tu woh filum dekha kya? Stree!*" Tembe nods and repeats the film's catchline. "*O stree, kal aana,*" he says, admitting that the horror-comedy gave him the shivers. "*Meri to phat gayee thi woh chudail ko dekh kar.*"

"That witch is like my Shanti—she scares me too," Todkar shudders.

Tembe, suddenly sober, wonders if there are ghosts and witches in Matheran too. Todkar laughs, mockingly exclaiming, "*Chaa*! *Kuchh nahi re,* wives turn into witches, but the rest is all hogwash. *Faltu ki baat* to scare people away. *Dekh* no lights are going to go off now..."

But they do. As they sit in the dark, Todkar tries to brazen it out. "And no one is going to come here with a *mombatti*." Almost on cue, a hand places a candle on the counter, making them both jump.

The bartender apologises, "Sorry sir, I didn't mean to scare you, but it's time for the bar to shut so we have put off the lights. You can finish your drink in the light of this candle and then go up to your suite. You can order room service there."

Todkar glares at him. "*Jaa re baba jaa,* I'm Insector Todkar from Mumbai and you are laying out the rules to me? The rule says this bar is open till 1 a.m. and it is just past 11 p.m. You can hoodwink the locals and the tourists but not me. No way am I going to pay double for a drink delivered to my room. I want my drink here and now. I am ordering you to make me one more peg."

Tembe, who is watching him with rounded eyes, raises a hand, reminding his boss that he could do with another whiskey and coke too. Todkar nods. "And one for him too. If you want to keep your job, you will do as I say. And switch on those damn lights now or your licence will be revoked," he hollers, his voice reverberating around the room.

He hopes somebody spreads the word. Else, he will have to make sure these lodges put up a notice laying down the timings. Bloody bartender, teaching him rules! He is going to have the rulebook thrown back at him now. Minutes later, the lights come on and Todkar smiles with satisfaction, saying, "Boss *hai re*." Tembe smiles back, happy to get more daaru.

The bartender sulks as he mixes their drinks and wonders when he will get home. His wife's name is also Shanti and she too can create a lot of ashanti. Besides, now he will have to make his way back in the dark, well past midnight. He shivers in his shoes, reminding himself not to go anywhere near Garbett or the railway tracks.

***

Cecil Lodge is in darkness, but in the adjourning villa, lights are streaming in from all the bedrooms on the first floor. In his room, Kiara is helping Sid change into his night clothes while urging him to brush his teeth properly if he doesn't want to lose them before he is forty. The little boy gives her a toothy grin, revealing two missing front teeth. He is unconcerned—forty is a lifetime away.

Right now, he just wants to tumble into bed. He has to wake up early, for Parzaan will be waiting. In the next room, the twins are preparing for bed too. Sana, looking out of the window, tells her sister that Matheran is a pretty cool place to spend the next few months. Sara grouses that she hates running around looking for a network and doesn't like the lodge much. "All those pictures in the dining room, they give me the creeps." She shivers, picking up her brush and trying to comb the tangles out of her hair.

Sana sees her struggling with the knots and comes back to sit on the bed. "Give me that brush, and let me do this for you before you tear all your hair out. Much as I like you, I don't want a bald twin." Both girls burst out laughing.

***

Aditya is stretched out on the bed in the master bedroom, making a mental checklist of all that needs to be done. The problem with old houses that have been shut for a while is that they need lots of time, care and money. Well, he can afford to lavish all three and turn this place into a home for his family and a home away from home for his guests. Right now though, there's no one at the property apart from the five of them, he says to himself in relief.

He is wrong. Downstairs, the knob on the main door turns from outside, with the door opening silently. The living room is in darkness. Someone steals across the wooden floor, checking out the three small rooms on the ground floor to see if the family which has just moved in has left their stamp on them.

The kitchenette hasn't been put to use yet, but the other two rooms are haphazardly stacked with cartons, with items of furniture scattered around. There are clothes and shoes strewn across the living room. It's a right royal mess.

In the darkness, there are some sounds of shuffling before the spectre goes up the stairs and steps back into the shadows as Kiara comes out of Sid's bedroom, looking around and wondering if she heard something just now. There's no one there except her. Perhaps she imagined it!

As she starts towards the stairs to get a bottle of water from below, her heart skips a beat. There's a shadow near the far wall, as if the devil is standing and watching her. She tiptoes towards it and laughs weakly when she discovers that it's a deer head mounted on the wall, the eyes beady and dead. That explains the horns!

As she turns away, the eyes suddenly come alive, observing her as she descends. When she reaches the living room, she fumbles along the wall till she reaches the switchboard. With one flick, light floods the room and she almost recoils in surprise. The room was messy when she left it. Now, it has been straightened out, as if someone came in after them and tidied up the place.

Kiara goes from room to room, appreciatively murmuring, "Who's my elf? Must be Aditya. I thought he was in the bedroom, but I guess he did all this before going up. And he did a great job too, which is surprising for him. Guess this place is turning him into a homebody. I was dreading getting up early and setting the house straight before the kids came back from their ride and added to the clutter."

There is a sudden sound from a window which has been left ajar. It makes her jump. When she moves closer to investigate, she laughs out loud again. "It's only the windchimes. No bells this time, just sticks hitting against each other. This old place is making me jittery."

She shuts the window, turns off the light and goes back up the stairs. As she turns towards the master bedroom, the door to the twins' room opens, and the girls along with Sid step out, giggling. Kiara frowns at Sid. "I thought you would be asleep by now."

He looks down, shuffling his feet. "I couldn't sleep." Realising that her baby is overexcited, she looks at Sara and Sana inquiringly. "If we play Scattergories, maybe he will calm down," Sana suggests.

Kiara nods, and with a whoop of delight, Aditya races into the master bedroom, shouting, "I am coming too." A ghostly figure watches them from the far end of the corridor. No one notices.

In the bedroom, Sana is laying down the rules, looking directly at Sid who tends to forget them. "You have two minutes to come up with an answer that you have to write down. Innovative answers will get ten points and common ones five. Got it?" When Sid nods, she snaps her fingers briskly, adding, "Okay, the timer starts now."

All five start writing furiously in response to her query about their best friend's name. Sid's answer, "Parzaan", makes his mother look at him curiously as she wonders about this friend whom she never heard of in Mumbai. Now, he can't stop talking about him. Where was he?

Sid looks out of the open door and straight at the boy in the kitchen. Only he can see him.

Sara asks the next question: "Your favourite food?" Kiara doesn't need to think, for it's Chinese—noodles, dim sums and chilli chicken. She has a sudden craving for her favourite meal and wonders if the chef can rustle up Chinese too.

Sara debates between pizza and frankie and chooses the latter. Her twin opts for Margherita pizza, while Aditya's pick is chicken *tikka*.

Once again, Sid has eyebrows rising when he reads out his answer: "Dhanshak." Sara points out that given that he ate it just that evening for the first time, it couldn't have become his favourite dish so quickly. The little boy insists he has always loved it. Aditya gives him 10 marks for innovation. His cousin sulks, complaining that he is just making things up so that he can win the game. He protests loudly. The third question is favourite festival. There's Eid, Holi, Diwali and Christmas. Sid is silent. Kiara prods, "Can't decide between Holi and Diwali, Siddie?" He mutters, "17th August." Sara smirks, "It's 15th August, dumbo, and Independence Day is not a festival." Sid looks towards the door for a long moment and then repeats, "17th August."

Suddenly worried, Kiara pulls him close and cuddles him. She's relieved when the next question is "your birth year". Sid never forgets the date or the year. But tonight it seems he has, for he mutters, "2015…17th August."

This time, Sara loses her temper and snaps, "If you don't want to play, say so. But do you have to spoil the game for us with your lies? It's innovation that gets you points, not imagination."

The little boy hides his face in his mother's bosom and bursts into tears at Sara's angry tone. Kiara picks him up and tells the others to excuse them—she will put Sid to sleep. She heads towards the door. Once outside, she's surprised when her son points straight ahead, saying, "There's a balcony that way. Let's go out for a minute and look at the stars."

She's surprised that he has explored the place on his own—normally, when he is somewhere new, he waits to do it with the family. But since they arrived at Cecil, he's doing everything on his own.

Sid wriggles out of her arms and runs towards the far end of the corridor with the familiarity of an inmate. He opens a door and a blast of cold air blows in as he runs out onto the balcony, gazing at the distant lights.

His mother smiles as she goes and stands beside him, pointing to one of the lights and saying, "I think that's our home in Mumbai." Sid shakes his head. "This is my home." Kiara shivers as a spider, big, hairy and black, crawls up the wall.

In the twins' bedroom, Aditya is looking down at the paper on which Sid has written his answers. He is frowning. All have some reference to Parsis. Weird! The girls are also talking about Sid's strange behaviour.

On the balcony, Kiara, her voice soft and gentle, asks Sid how he knows about this terrace. He points to the yard below, telling her that he was playing there that evening. She remembers him racing around with the cycle handle and says, smiling, "Do you like it out here or are you missing your friends, Siddie?" He seems surprised by the question. "Why would I miss them? Parzaan is here with me."

Taking him by the hand, Kiara leads him out and towards his bedroom. She has no idea if this Parzaan is dead or alive. If he is still in this world, why is he hiding? She must have a word with Aditya about Sid. He has never let his imagination take flight like this before.

Must be the pandemic, she concludes. It had locked people in their homes for months at a stretch. Many had found imaginary friends to stay sane. The three of them had been cut off even from the twins and their family despite living quite close to each other. That's when Sid had started talking to himself for hours and she had let him because there was so much to do. Was that when he found Parzaan?

As they walk down the corridor, someone walks behind them, whispering a nursery rhyme…

Little Miss Muffet,
Sat on her tuffet,

Eating her curds and whey,
Along came a big spider
And sat down beside her,
Frightening Miss Muffet away.

Kiara doesn't hear, but Sid turns back and worriedly looks for the spider. Thankfully, he can't spot it.

They enter his bedroom, and a few minutes later, he has been tucked into bed. The lights go off.

Almost simultaneously, the lights in one of the rooms in Cecil Lodge switch on. It's room no. 19.

8

Love, Sex & Terror

In the master bedroom, Kiara steps out of the washroom in sexy red lingerie. Only a night lamp is on, which illuminates a hump under the quilt. As she pads softly towards the bed, she wonders if Aditya has fallen asleep. He must be exhausted, for it's been a long day, but she had hoped that they would…

Suddenly, a pair of hands encircle her from behind and pull her back. Terrified, Kiara opens her mouth, but a hand cups it, cutting off her scream. Her blood turns cold and her eyes flit wildly as the other hand slowly moves down her body, caressing her.

Kiara struggles to break free from the tight grasp. Despite her frail appearance, she is strong. Plus, she has talons. She draws blood and, with a muffled oath, the man who has accosted her turns her around, somewhat roughly, to face him. She blinks in astonishment.

It's Aditya. Before she can say a word, his lips cover hers and his hands gently push her back towards the bed. She tumbles into it and he joins her. "I thought you were sleeping," she murmurs as his lips travel down, nipping and nuzzling.

He looks up with a throaty laugh. "I might as well be dead if I go to sleep tonight—our first night in our new home. It feels like our *suhaag raat*—the first night of our marriage. Now, where were we before you interrupted me so rudely to talk about sleep. I'm sorry, *biwi,* I have better things to do than talk right now."

She giggles and he gets back to the task of arousing her. A few moments later, Kaira sighs under the skillful hands of her husband and admits, "I won't lie, not when you are driving me crazy like this. I was hoping we would do..." She gasps as his teeth bite into her soft skin. By way of apology, Aditya licks the spot tenderly but doesn't stop.

They make love, slowly, in a sensuous tangle of limbs. The moon peeps in and showers its sheen on them. The room is silent except for the occasional sounds of gentle kisses, soft reprimands, careless whispers and sighs of satisfaction amid the growing need for more.The sheets twist, the comforter is thrown aside and the pillows are kicked to the floor as the pace of their love-making turns more frenzied and their excitement mounts. The bed shakes, the moon vanishes and Kiara climaxes with a muffled scream, followed by Aditya's satiated grunt. Spent and sweaty, he cuddles her.

For a while, they are both content and happy, enjoying this moment of intimacy. Then, as the moon returns, Aditya notices the worried look in his wife's eyes and, leaning down for a kiss, asks her what troubles her. "I hope I haven't come up short, else I will have to scale up my performance before the night is out?" he teases and is surprised when she doesn't rise to the bait. Knowing her well, he waits patiently for her to confide in him.

After long minutes, Kiara hesitatingly brings up the subject of their son that has been bothering her. "Sid's been behaving rather strangely since we entered Cecil, you must have noticed," she points out. When he nods, she goes on to narrate how on the balcony a little while ago, he had claimed that this was his home.

"I am happy to see how well he has adapted to the quiet hills after the cacophony of the city, but adopting dead people is a bit much. And then there is this Parzaan whom he keeps calling out to. He must live in the vicinity. I'm surprised that except for Sid, no one else has seen him," she says. Aditya remembers the boy's answers while playing the game—everything was linked to Parsis and a family they knew nothing about. He wonders whether to share this with Kaira but decides not to scare her. She is already upset and he doesn't want her to start thinking negatively of this beautiful property and demand to be taken back home to Mumbai. In a way, he endorses what Sid had told her earlier. This was their home now.

"Don't overthink. Kids sometimes behave strangely and in a way we adults will never understand. Sid is excited—it's a new place and there is so much space for him to play," Aditya reasons.

He reminds her that their son's teachers used to constantly tell them that he had an overactive imagination. "That's not a bad thing really. He is using it now to spin stories around this place. It's empty except for us and perhaps he is lonely. In Mumbai, his friends were always walking in and out of our home. Here he has no one besides his cousins, who, being twins, are a unit. So, he is making up friends like Parzaan," he explains to his wife.

He recalls their meal in the dining room and how Sid had come up with names for some of the oldies in the portraits.

"He's innovative, if nothing else," he laughs and drops a kiss on Kiara's furrowed forehead before moving his lips to her eyes, nose and mouth.

She snuggles against him, feeling safe and settled in his arms. He wraps his arms around her. Suddenly, tiredness washes over him. Within minutes he is asleep, snoring softly. She smiles looking into the face of the man she has loved forever.

But her smile vanishes soon as her thoughts reel back to their child. "This is a beautiful place, but we need to know something about its history and those who lived here before us. And I must find out where Parzaan lives and maybe meet his mamma," she murmurs, finally nodding off.

In the living room, the clock strikes 12.

***

Charlotte Lake and the temple near it are shimmering in the silvery moonlight. Everything is serene and beautifully so. Then, suddenly, a black horse trots out of the jungle and takes the road leading to Cecil Lodge.

Madhu watches him from behind the trees, waiting till the horse disappears from view, before going back into the forest.

***

In the campus, the swings are in motion. No one notices.

***

Towards dawn, Aditya wakes up and wanders to the window. Looking out, he sees that the campus is still dark, though the sky is beginning to clear. The illuminated dial of the clock reads 4 a.m. It's so blissfully quiet here…and chilly.

He rubs his arms and quickly heads back to bed. Looking down at a sleeping Kiara, he remembers their lovemaking. If only she would wake up, they could pick up where they had left off!

But Kiara's lost in a dream, and it is not pleasant from the expression on her face and the way her eyelids are fluttering. She suddenly calls out to someone to "stop", murmuring her protest. She's mumbling about trains and tunnels now. Aditya gently strokes her hair, wondering how to reassure his wife that all is well. Tomorrow he will ask Madhu if he knows of a little boy called Parzaan who lives around the lodge, he decides.

***

In the living room below, in the light of a lone lamp, a lady is sitting in the rocking chair. Her face is covered in shadows as she says, "You must be happy now, Parzaan. You finally have a friend!"

***

As sunlight streams into the curtainless room, Kiara wakes up with a start. She notices instantly that Aditya is not beside her. The house is silent—too silent.

She picks up the robe which Aditya has laid on the chair and wraps it on. She walks to the washroom and, in the mirror over the washbasin, sees a purplish bruise on her neck. A love bite. She smiles, mumbling, "I will need makeup to hide the signs of Aditya's passion. I wonder where he has disappeared. From the way he was going last night, I had expected him to wake me up early and…"

Monkeys are running berserk on the roof. Thud, thud, thud...They are making a racket. Ever the protective mamma, Kiara quickly heads towards the kids' rooms. Sid's room is empty and so is the twins' bedroom.

Alarmed, she walks down the stairs. The living room is also empty, though the lamp by the rocking chair is on. The window beside it is also open. Didn't I shut it last night, wonders Kiara. Maybe Aditya came down to read and forgot to shut it. After all, he is still new to the place.

Kiara calls out to her family and is greeted with silence. She is beginning to get anxious when she remembers that Suresh bhai was supposed to take them to Sunrise Point early that morning. She dials Aditya but his phone is off. She tries Suresh bhai's cell, but she can't get through to him either. Damn the network! She hopes that they are safe, for she has this funny feeling...

Too wired up to sleep, she steps out and heads towards the lodge. Maybe the caretaker is back or at least the helper might be. What did Aditya say his name was? It probably didn't even register in her mind as she hasn't seen him yet. The campus has been deserted since their arrival.

Kiara suddenly realises that she's in a robe with very little beneath it and hurriedly turns towards the villa. But it is as if something, or rather someone, is pushing her towards the main gate, propelling her in that direction with a hand against the small of her back. She resists it a while before eventually surrendering to the superior power.

Upon reaching the gate, Kiara unlatches it and walks down the deserted road. Suddenly, she hears the sound of a horse's hooves and turns to see it. There's no horse, but as she walks further ahead, she can hear the faint honking of a train from a distance. Kiara begins to run towards it, driven by the same force. Her mind is blank. The robe flutters against the wind around her as she races.

Once in a while, she stumbles and falls but picks herself up and continues running. Her mouth is open. She is screaming for Aditya, Sana, Sara and Sid but no sounds come out.

As she nears the station, she can see a figure on the tracks. She races towards it, unmindful of the approaching train. Her attention is completely focussed on the person in front of her. The figure looks like a woman's and is holding something in her hands. She can't see the stranger's face, but she has this uncanny feeling that their lives are interlinked in an incomprehensible but intimate way.

Kiara keeps running till she is knocked down by the train.

9

A Close Shave

At Cecil Lodge, Suresh is helping the girls mount their horses. It's still dark outside and deserted. The ghodawallah hands Sara and Sana their helmets. The twins quickly wear them, fastening the straps. Suresh smiles his approval and then turns to his assistant, Suraj, who is tightening the straps on Sid's helmet. Taking no chances, he tugs on them to ensure that they are secure before checking on their saddles one more time.

Aditya, sitting astride his horse and impatient to be gone, laughs at him. "Stop fussing, Suresh bhai. Everything is fine. Give us the green signal now, so we can start our ride before the sun goes up."

Suresh grins sheepishly, admitting that the recent events and accidents have left the locals shaken. "Just two days ago, a babu from Mumbai...*Ab kya naam tha unka*?" He frowns as he tries to recall the man's name. Suraj remembers it for him and he nods. *"Haan haan,* Shah. Well, the babu fell off his horse and died."

Aditya nods soberly. "Yes, I know. Dasturi Naka was crawling with TV reporters yesterday when we arrived."

"Police too," Suraj mutters, looking unhappy. Cops could be a bother at the best of times, and now an inspector had come down from Mumbai with his aide to look into the babu's accidental death. Rahim chacha and Rashid had been questioned for hours. Now, everyone was wondering who would be pulled in next, with some like his cousin Chandu saying that if the police were not happy with your answers, they would beat you black and blue. "Poor guy," Aditya is saying sympathetically, adding, *"Par gira kaise woh?"*

Suresh shakes his head. "No idea, baba. He left his sons with Rahim chacha and Rashid and went racing off alone. He was no novice. He had been coming to Matheran for over a decade and was an experienced rider. They were on their way to Sunrise Point, but everyone thinks the babu took the left turn towards Garbett and that spooked the horse."

Suraj continues the narration, explaining that since the road to Garbett had recently been closed for repairs after a landslide, presumably Shah couldn't go all the way up and instead came down riding towards the railway tracks before turning back in the same direction until the fatal fall. "He died like the other one...*Bhoot hai wahan.*"

Sara, who has been listening intently, abruptly pipes up, "*Bhoot*...You mean a ghost?" Aditya suddenly realises that they are not alone. Not wanting the twins to be spooked by local gossip, he decides to change the topic. Pointing to the reddening sky, he says, "Come on, kids. We need to pick up our pace if we want to catch the sunrise."

Sid, cranky perhaps because he has been woken so early, is whining that Google has disappeared again. "Maybe Parzaan took him," he mumbles.

Aditya, who is holding him securely in front of him, remembers how disturbed Kiara was last night about his imaginary buddy and decides that it's time to nip this friendship in the bud. But he will wait till later to do that. For now, he simply says, "I think Google just wandered off towards the woods to go potty. He doesn't have a washroom like you do."

His son laughs, amused by the idea. If they had looked back they would have seen the mutt sitting near the gate, watching their disappearing figures. The animal now turns and walks back towards the lodge.

***

A couple of minutes later, Madhu walks into the compound and hurries towards the villa to report to Aditya. He debates whether to ring the bell or to knock. Undecided, he gives the door a push with his right foot and is surprised when it swings open soundlessly. He enters and scopes out the living room. The rocking chair is still moving, as if someone was sitting in it and has just vacated it. He looks around for Aditya or anyone else. The house is quiet and no one seems to be around.

He notices the open window near the chair and decides it's the breeze that is making it sway. But the door was open, so there must be someone around.

He strolls towards the kitchenette. It's not been used. He wanders towards the two other rooms on the ground floor, peeping into bags and opening boxes before taking the stairs.

As he walks up, the woman who had been sitting in the rocking chair suddenly appears and watches him ascend. You can see her face clearly now—it's the lady from the portrait in the dining room cradling the infant whom Sid had christened Parzaan Dastoor Irani the previous evening.

Madhu reaches the first floor and takes a quick tour of the twins' bedroom. He sniffs at a bottle of perfume, picks up

Sana's earplugs to try them on and spots Sara's still plugged-in charger and pockets it.

Sid's bedroom is next—Madhu finishes a bottle of mineral water and strolls towards the master bedroom. The door is open and he stops short as Kiara screams in her sleep. He waits till she is quiet again before tiptoeing to stand at the threshold of the bedroom, watching her thrash around in the double bed. She is obviously having a nightmare.

As she moves around restlessly, the comforter slips off. She is in her lingerie and his eyes almost pop out of his head as he gawks at the creamy flesh and inches closer, making sure not to wake her up. He hurriedly retreats a few steps when Kiara shouts out a name. Then, suddenly, all the fight seems to go out of her and she lies still and inert.

Madhu walks right up and stands by the bed, looking down at her. He leans forward when a sudden sound from the door makes him freeze. He turns, his eyes wide and frightened. There's no one there though he could have sworn that someone was watching him from the door. He can still feel those eyes on him. He races towards the adjoining balcony.

There is a loud thumping sound, like monkeys jumping on the roof. Kiara wakes up looking disconcerted and takes in her surroundings. Remembering she is in Matheran, she gets out of the bed even as Madhu drops to the ground from the balcony.

As he tries to stand up, he grimaces in pain, realising he has sprained his ankle. "Damn, I should not have gone into the house like that! I should have knocked, rung the bell, called the sahab. But the door was open and how could I know that the memsahib was alone? She had been dreaming…more like a nightmare…She had shouted a name…But how could she know?"

The sound of footsteps alerts him to the fact that Kiara is walking out. He doesn't want her to discover him. How will he explain what he is doing there? He could lose his job? Hobbling painfully, he heads towards the back of the house just as Kiara steps out.

She looks out at the deserted campus, which is lit up by the rays of the rising sun. Suddenly, with a volley of barks, Google races towards the villa. The dog makes Kiara smile as she walks back inside and heads towards the washroom.

In the mirror, above the basin, she checks out her appearance. The nightmare is still clinging to her and she looks pale and peaky. She inspects to see if she has hurt herself anywhere, The dream had felt so real. She can still feel the pain of running along the tracks, tripping and falling. But there is not even a scratch on her. All she can see is a love bite blooming at the nape of her neck. That is Aditya's doing.

She smiles, remembering their night of passion, and returns to the bedroom. Picking up her cellphone from the bedside table, she starts scrolling through her WhatsApp chats. Sonal wants to know how the kids are doing. Her mother is worried about what they are eating. Their nana wants her to send a picture of the kids riding. Her husband has also left her a message. "I love you, Sleeping Beauty. Wanted to kiss you before I left for Sunrise Point with the kids, but didn't want to wake you. If you did, I might have missed the ride, so I'm taking a rain check until tonight."

Kiara's smile blooms and she tries to call her husband. "No network as usual," she sighs.

***

Aditya is riding through the woods, mesmerised by his surroundings. The first rays of the sun stream through the dense foliage, lighting up the darkness. The silence is absolute here—no monkeys chattering or birds chirping; just the clip cop of the horse shoes. Even Sid, perhaps influenced by the surroundings, is mercifully quiet. Perhaps he has nodded off. Aditya's arms tighten around the child even as his thoughts drift to his wife.

"This is so beautiful and romantic. I must come here alone with Kiara. It would make us feel like we were on our honeymoon again," he thinks, smiling as he looks down at the blanket of fallen leaves. "And that's a great place to make love." The twins with the ghodawallahs have fallen back. Lost in his thoughts, Aditya lets the big, white horse he is riding take the lead. At the junction, Badal moves to the left even as Suresh's voice reaches Aditya through his meanderings. "Right *lena,* baba. Take right to Sunrise Point."

Before he can rein in the horse, Badal has moved towards Garbett Point. The sun is blotted out by the trees, and while it was tranquil down below, there is a sense of foreboding as they climb the hill. He can hear the faint sound of the train honking and someone calling out to him. Even Sid is beginning to move restlessly against him.

Aditya struggles with the horse. Badal is not as strong as Bingo and after a brief tug-of-war, he turns towards the junction where Suresh and Suraj are standing with the twins and the horses, looking in the direction of Garbett Point, with their faces wearing expressions of dread.

Suraj lets out a whoop when he spots Aditya, pointing him out to Suresh, who sighs with relief. "Thank God!" When Aditya draws closer he admonishes mildly, "Baba, I told you not to take the left turn. That road is closed."

Aditya is looking dazed. "The train. Did you hear it?" Suresh starts, "What train? No train is expected for another hour."

Aditya shakes his head—he had heard it honking clearly. As they trot up, he remembers the voice shouting for help. It sounded just like Kiara's. Suresh bhai is looking at him worriedly.

***

In the bungalow, Kiara is stepping out of the shower. Suddenly, she freezes. Since she was alone in the house, she had not bothered to shut the door. It is now ajar and through the crack, she can see a pair of eyes. Swallowing past the lump in her throat, she calls out in a thin, quivering voice. "*Kaun hai*? I ask again, who's there?"

Instantly, the person standing at the opposite side of the door retreats. She can actually feel the presence leaving the room. Wrapping the towel more tightly around her, Kiara steps out into the bedroom, which appears to be empty. Shivering as much from the cold as from apprehension, she walks out into the corridor, wondering if the kids are back. Though none of them would have stood quietly watching her. Not even Aditya.

Still she raises her voice, "Sid…Sara…Sana…Aditya...Hey, are you guys home?" She is greeted with silence, but down the corridor, in the long mirror facing her, she sees a faint image that draws her forward. When she is closer, she almost screams out loud as she sees a half-naked woman holding a towel tightly to hide her modesty.

Rubbing her eyes, she looks again. This time she bursts out laughing. It is her own reflection. "God, I must be reeling from the nightmare still, seeing someone else there instead of me. I wonder if I imagined the eyes too…"

She heads down the stairs. The house is empty, but the main door is open. Frowning, she shuts it. She could have sworn that she had locked it last night. Maybe one of the kids didn't shut it properly on their way out. She makes a mental note to speak to her family about their habit of leaving front doors open even if there was no one around for miles.

As she walks up again, the rocking chair turns towards the stairs and starts moving on its own. It's as if someone is sitting on it, watching her. Invisible eyes, intent and unblinking.

10

A Coughing Fit

Aditya and the kids have reached Sunrise Point. The horses have been tied to the trees. Suraj is pointing to the ball of fire which seems to be coming out of the mountains, making sure the girls are not standing too close to the iron railing and that the little boy's hand is firmly in his own. Suresh watches them for a moment and then quietly slides up to Aditya, who is looking at the sunrise but not really seeing it, his mind still on the train and the cries of help he thought he heard back near Garbett Point.

"Baba, can I ask you something if you don't mind?" Suresh asks hesitatingly, and Aditya turns to him, forcing a smile to his lips. "Of course, what do you want to know?"

Suresh waits a beat and then blurts out, "Why did you buy Cecil Lodge? I mean, have you really bought it yet or…"

He trails off as a flicker of irritation crosses Aditya's face. "I told you why yesterday. It's my business," he snaps. Noticing a strange expression on the ghodawallah's face, he prods, "What's the problem, man? Since I landed here yesterday, I've been getting this feeling that there's something fishy about the lodge that I don't know about. Tell me what it is without beating around the bush now. Give it to me straight."

Suresh doesn't answer immediately. Aditya can see that he is debating how much to reveal. He keeps his eyes on the man who is kicking some stones around with his scruffy sneakers. Finally, he mumbles, "Baba, if you haven't bought the place yet, I urge you not to do so. And if you already have, please don't stay there with bhabhi-ji and the bachchas. *Jagah sahi nahi hai*. Go back to Mumbai."

Aditya is seriously concerned now but tries not to show it. "Why shouldn't I stay there?" he demands, somewhat aggressively.

Suresh finally meets his eyes, looking distraught. "Well, it's been closed for a while since..."

But he's cut off before he can say more. Shrugging off Suraj's restraining hand, Sid runs to his father, whining, "Papa, I want to go home now. I want to play with Parzaan. He's calling me."

At the mention of Parzaan's name, Suresh looks shocked and urges, "Baba, let's go back. Now, please."

Aditya is bemused. It is understandable that Sid is getting bored, but why would the horseman try to hurry him up, he wonders. Suresh can see the questions on his face and tries to speak but a bout of coughing stops him. Aditya hands him his water bottle, patting him on the back and saying, "Now now, relax. Drink some water."

Suresh takes a big gulp. He tries to speak again but is felled by another coughing fit. The others have noticed the situation and Suraj comes running with the girls. "Chacha, *kya hua?* What's wrong?" he asks.

Sara and Sana are looking at Suresh, wide-eyed. The man is almost doubled over, holding his throat and gasping as if someone is strangling him.

"Drink some more water," Aditya coaxes, pushing the bottle into his hands. Sid stands beside him, whining, "Come on, Papa. I want to play with Parzaan."

***

Now fully dressed, Kiara walks out of the bungalow. She notices Madhu walking towards the lodge. She beckons him over. For a minute, it seems like he will not answer her. Realising that he could get into trouble if he doesn't, he finally drags his feet and heads in her direction, wondering apprehensively if she had spotted him in the house.

He now understands that Kiara is looking at him. She must have asked him a question. He has no idea what it is and looks at her blankly. Figuring that the guy is a little slow, she repeats her query, "How long have you been here?"

His response—"forever"—makes her glance at him sharply. So he elaborates, "I mean, I was born in Matheran..."

Kiara shakes her head with a laugh. "No, I meant here. How long have you been working at Cecil Lodge?"

His eyes dart up to meet hers and he replies, "Since a few months."

Kiara is suddenly conscious of the fact that besides the two of them, there's no one around. "Who else lives here? Is there a boy called Parzaan in the vicinity?" she prods.

Suddenly edgy, he mutters, "I don't know anything," and walks away before she can utter another word. Kiara wonders if she should follow him into the house and prod him some more. A sudden gust of wind makes her shiver despite the warmth of the bright sun shining above. She wonders when Aditya and the kids will be home and makes an impulsive resolve. Next time, she will go riding with them even if it means sacrificing her sleep.

***

Aditya and his party of five have stopped at a small roadside dhaba. While the girls are biting into omelette-*pav* with relish, Sid is sulking in a corner. He wants to be home, playing with Parzaan—why can't anyone get that!

His father is bent over Suresh, who is looking really ill. As if in high fever, the ghodawallah is shivering and coughing in short bursts that leave him gasping. Suraj is standing beside him looking concerned.

Aditya, who is trying to coax Suresh to have some hot tea, reprimands the boy. "If you knew Suresh bhai was so unwell, why didn't you stop him from coming today? We are not tourists. We are going to be in Matheran for a while. We could have gone to Sunrise Point another day; there was no tearing hurry to visit."

Suraj stammers, "*Par,* babu, he was fine when we left…In fact, he seemed okay right till we reached Sunrise…"

Coughing, Suresh nods. "Yes, I was fine…I am fine. Really, I am, baba. Don't worry."

Suraj can see that Aditya is not convinced and he frowns darkly at Suresh. "You would be fine if you only stopped drinking. *Bahut peene lage ho,* chacha. Chachi keeps telling you to stop, but you don't even listen to her. *Isiliye to aaj yeh halat hai aapka.*" He throws his hands up in exasperation.

Aditya suddenly figures that Suresh could be suffering from alcohol withdrawal symptoms and sternly tells him, "Since when have you started drinking so much, Suresh bhai? You never used to before. We can all see that it is taking a toll on your health."

The twins have finished eating and are posing for selfies, pouting and smiling for their cellphone cameras. They call out to Sid to join the photo session. Disgruntled, he shakes his head and mutters, "I don't know why we are wasting time here. Back home, Parzaan is getting impatient."

Meanwhile, Suresh, who is trying to play down his sudden illness, begins coughing again. Aditya holds up a hand to stop him from speaking. "No, don't say anything more. The boy in the market mentioned that you began drowning your sorrows in alcohol after that fire in your stable cost you four horses. Accidents happen, bhai. We all have lost a lot of money—some even their livelihood—during the pandemic. You can't let yourself go to pieces like this. Animals can be replaced."

Suraj points out that they don't like losing horses. "They are not just our livelihood, babu. They are our family. Now Bingo is gone. No one has seen him since the accident. Rahim chacha is distraught. Goats and chicken have also been disappearing from our yards, and we sometimes find them slaughtered in the woods near Cecil. God alone knows what is happening! *Kitni shanti thi yahan. Ab jaise kisi ki nazar lag gayi hai.* An evil eye is on us," he wails.

Suresh shivers and starts coughing again.

***

On a restaurant balcony on Matheran's Mall Road, an old man is smoking a hookah while the two cops, Todkar and Tembe, are having breakfast.

"*Bhurji mast hai*, sahib. Spicy! Lots of green chillies mixed in with tomatoes, onions and coriander, which is just the way I like my eggs. And this *pav*," says Tembe as he picks up the last bun and regards it lovingly, "It is *ekdum* bakery *ka* fresh."

He offers it to Todkar, but the inspector burps, shakes his head and gently pats his paunch. "No, you finish it. I am stuffed. If Shanti was here, she would have started her lecture by now." He mimics his wife's voice. "*Kitna khate ho*? Why do you always have to overeat? *Mote ho rahe ho. Gym bhi nahin jaate ho.* Look at me, *ekdum* slim and sexy. I never miss my morning walks and Zumba classes."

Tembe laughs as he dunks the *pav* in his tea. "Sir, *aap* bhabhi-ji *se bahut pyaar karte ho, bole to ekdum* I love you, Shanti. Even here, far away from the city and her, you can only think of your Shanti."

Todkar guffaws and punches him. "*Bahut maskari karne laga hai re tu.* Always pulling my leg. Don't forget I am your boss."

Tembe immediately jumps up and smartly salutes him. The inspector pushes him back to his seat and, looking in the direction of the old man, says, "So, Khan sahab, I've been told that your lodge and this restaurant are the oldest properties in Matheran."

Khan retorts, "It's one of the oldest, not the oldest—that's Cecil Lodge. It once belonged to Irani sahab—Faroukh Dinyar Irani—and in its time, the lodge was very popular with tourists, for it was known for its simple, clean rooms and exquisite Parsi cuisine, with Shahnaz beti overseeing everything with her father and Shivaji." He stops abruptly and puffs on his hookah.

Todkar looks at him curiously. "You seem to know a lot about Cecil?"

Khan says shortly, "My wife used to work there once."

The inspector drains his cup of tea and stands up, stating, "Well, it has a new owner now, I am told." Using a toothpick to dig food remnants out of the furrows between his teeth, he asks, "Khan sahab, what do you think happened to Manish Shah, the businessman from Mumbai who fell to his death?"

A voice calls out from inside a room, "It's because of *her*. We have to stop *her*. She is angry and dangerous."

The voice is that of Sumaila, Khan's wife. An elderly lady, with long, white hair around a thin, almost skeletal face, emerges from the room, muttering, "Send those people away. They can't stay here. They are in danger."

Khan shouts to his daughter. "Shazia…Shazia…Shazia… Take your mother inside and give her the pills."

When Shazia doesn't answer him, Khan laboriously gets to his feet, and holding his wife firmly by the elbow, he steers her towards the room, gently pushing her inside and latching the door from outside.

The two cops have been watching keenly, and as Khan settles down with his hookah again, the inspector asks, "What's wrong with her?"

The old man takes his time before answering, finally saying in a gruff voice, "*Pata nahin,* sahab. She speaks nonsense all day. *Hosh mein nahi rehti aaj kal.* She was normal till…" his voice trails off miserably.

Todkar prods, "She mentioned someone angry and dangerous just now, who had to be stopped. *Kiski baat kar rahin thi*?"

Khan shrugs dismissively. "Who knows! Sumaila lives in her own world now, where reality and fantasy overlap. To get back to your question, our family has been living here for the last 100 years, maybe more. It's a nice place—*taaza hawa* and lots of tourists. Most don't stay longer than a few days but go back home refreshed. Lonavala, Mahabaleshwar, Goa, *sab* develop *ho gaye hain*, but here in Matheran, there are no signs of development. *Chalo, hum khush hain…*"

Tembe reminds him that the inspector was asking about the recent death and Khan looks into the distance. "People are dying all over the world due to Corona. This one was an accident as the horse was out of control. Why make a mountain out of a molehill?" he says thoughtfully.

Todkar nods. "*Baat to sahi hai,* Khan sahab. This Coronavirus has made all our lives hell. Thank God we have got our two vaccine jabs now and can go back to an uneasy normal."

From inside the latched room, the sounds of things being flung around and the door being banged on can be heard. Sumaila is wanting to get out. The concerned cops look towards the closed door. Khan continues to smoke his hookah placidly and unconcerned.

When it is evident that the man won't say anything more, Todkar gestures to Tembe that it's time they were off. The constable gets up and the inspector turns to the owner, saying, "Okay, Khan sahab. *Phir milte hain.* You take good care of the missus."

The old man nods and graciously replies, "*Phir aana,* sahab. Next time I will get Shazia to make kebabs for you."

Tembe licks his lips in anticipation.

As they are on their way down the stairs, the cops run into Khan's daughter who hurries past without a word. They walk out into the street and Todkar stops at a paan bidi shop right across from the restaurant for cigarettes. They have an uninterrupted view of the balcony and he can see Khan shouting and gesturing angrily at Shazia. The inspector watches father and daughter, and as Tembe comes up with the cigarettes, he softly muses, "There's something weird going on with Khan's wife. *Kuch toh gadbad hai.* She knows something that they don't want to come out. We will have to get to the bottom of this."

His aide looks towards the balcony. Sensing their scrutiny, Khan turns in their direction, starts and says something to Shazia. Together, they disappear into the room where he has locked up his wife.

11

Mirror Image

Kiara is standing in front of the washbasin with a hair dryer in her hand, looking for an electric socket to plug it in. She finds one and inserts it, flicking on the switch. There's a loud, grating sound, like a drilling machine, followed by a spark before the dryer dies out. Sighing over the fuse, she contemplates her wet hair and walks into the bedroom and out to the balcony, hoping to spot Aditya.

She sees Madhu instead, walking towards the lodge. "I could ask him if there's a dryer in there or an adapter maybe," she muses and runs down the stairs and out again. He has disappeared into the lodge. She follows him. It is dark and silent inside. She walks swiftly down the corridor, peeping into the rooms and scanning the dining room and the smoker's lounge. There is no trace of the man. The kitchen window faces the back of the property, and through it, she sees Madhu disappearing into the woods. "Why would he go there now? I must remember to ask him when I see him next," she notes to herself, frowning and irritated, as she walks back to the villa.

As soon as she enters, a thudding sound from the first floor attracts her attention. It sounds like someone is opening and closing a door. Following the sound, Kiara runs up the stairs. She can hear the faint tinkle of windchimes and wonders when Aditya put them up. The sound is coming from near the terrace Sid had led her to last night.

As she walks towards it, the sounds die away. Frowning, she peers at the wall and sees a door cut in it so cleverly that it is almost invisible. Had it not been for the sounds, she would have never noticed it.

Kiara runs her hand over the wall and finds a button and pushes it. A door swings open silently and she steps into another bedroom. This must be where Sid found the cycle handle, she conjectures as she looks at the boxes scattered around. She smiles. The room is lit by a lone bulb, which gives the space an eerie red glow. She wonders who switched it on.

There is a big bed in the centre, and a huge mirror screwed to the wall at one end of the room. Opposite it is a wardrobe, its door slightly ajar, as if inviting her to take a look. She almost floats towards it, soon rummaging through the clothes hung up inside with curiosity and delight. Kiara loves clothes and these are good stuff, the kind she would pick up herself.

She pulls out a few of the dresses, holding them against her and looking at her reflection in the mirror. They look good. She particularly likes a white off-shoulder dress, which is almost like a gown. It's made of chiffon and clearly meant for a special occasion. Taking off her T-shirt, she slips on the dress, kicking off her jeans and sneakers as well in the process. Instantly, her personality changes.

She looks younger as she twirls before the mirror, laughing girlishly. She opens a drawer and hunts through it with a familiarity which would have been disconcerting to someone watching her. She finally digs out a lipstick, removes the cap and colours her lips a deep scarlet.

She then finds a mascara, eye-shadow and eye-liner in the same drawer and starts making up her face. Slowly, her face transmutes from Kiara's to that of the woman in the black-and-white portrait in the dining room who has been frequenting the house. It then changes back to Kiara's, as if these are dual personalities of the same person.

Kiara seems to be in a trance as she smiles sexily into the mirror, running her hands over her body and humming a song. Suddenly, there's the sound of horses, followed by the chatter of children. Though faint, Kiara is instantly alert, her smile fading away.

***

At the gate of Cecil Lodge, Suraj is helping the kids disembark. As soon as he is off the horse, Sid races inside without a word to anyone. Aditya looks after him with a displeased expression. In just two days, the boy is turning into a brat, forgetting his Ps and Qs. The twins thank Suraj and run after Sid. He is headed towards the lodge instead of the bungalow. They call out to him, but he doesn't even turn.

Looking pale and feverish, Suresh is leaning weakly against the gate. Taking out a few hunderd-rupee notes, Aditya looks at him, concern writ large on his face. "Suresh bhai, you don't look well. Why don't you come in for a while, both Suraj and you can have some breakfast with us before you return home. I would have preferred it if you had gone back directly from the dhaba, but you insisted on coming. Now that you are here..."

Suresh interrupts him, his voice low and hoarse from the coughing. "I had to. It was my responsibility to see you back home safe. But now...now I have to go home." He starts coughing again.

Aditya turns to Suraj and says, "Suraj, make sure you get Suresh bhai back home safe. And if you need anything, anything at all, call me. Understand? Meanwhile, get him a doctor." The younger boy nods, his eyes fixed on the lodge. Suresh bhai entreats him, his hands folded in prayer and a strange look in his eyes. "Leave, baba. Leave this place. Now."

Disturbed, Aditya folds his hands over the horseman's and softly says, "Don't worry about me, bhai. I'm fine. You take care of yourself and get well soon. We need to take many more trips together."

He pushes the money into Suresh's hands, who looks at the notes with a surprised face. "But this is more than..." Suddenly, his eyes drift towards the balcony. Kiara is standing there in a white dress. Suresh freezes. In his mind, he sees flashes of another woman wearing the same dress. He tries to say something, but no words come out.

Sid has run out of the lodge and is careening around the grounds at full speed, screaming, "Parzaan...Parzaan..."

Suresh stares at him, as if he has seen a ghost. Suddenly, he hears the sound of an approaching train and sees a woman running on railway tracks while holding something in her hands. She falls, gets up, stumbles and falls again.

The seesaw in the yard comes to a screeching stop. The swing is going up and down wildly. The merry-go-round is spinning, as if it has a mind of its own. Suresh looks at Aditya wondering why he can't see all this and feel his terror. The look on the other man's face is puzzled.

Aditya's confusion changes to surprise when Suresh suddenly jumps on one of the horses and rides away. Suraj calls out to him to stop. Then jumping on another horse and leading the other, he follows him.

Sid runs off towards the lodge, calling out to Parzaan. The twins watch as he brushes past them without a glance or a word, still screaming for Parzaan. Sara shrugs her shoulders. She's at a loss to explain her cousin's strange behaviour.

Kaira watches everything with a smile on her face.

***

At the Matheran railway station, four youngsters get off the train late in the afternoon. They are travel bloggers.

Zoya, a pretty girl in her twenties whose perfect-ten figure is wrapped in super skinny jeans and a lycra Tee, finger-combs a mass of windblown curls and outlines her pout with a dash of ruby-red lip colour as she takes a quick peek at the mirror the other girl is holding up for her. She then turns towards the camera, which one of the boys is operating. Speaking into it, she begins, "Hey, all you hot gals and cool dudes! Welcome to our YouTube channel and its new show, *Haunted*. If you haven't subscribed yet, do it now, before you are possessed!" Her eyes roll and she pretends to swoon.

Priya, small, mousy and always outshone by the vivacious Zoya, smothers a giggle, marvelling at her friend's ease before the lens. The girl is a star!

In a husky, seductive voice, Zoya now says, "Be sure to 'like' and post your comments as we go hunting for Matheran's top ten haunted spots. Are you shivering in your shoes yet? No? Well, I assure you, you will get the shakes soon. *Nahi toh* I am dead. Yes, DEAD. So, stay tuned and stick close by me over the next couple of days because we never know what we might find up here in the hills, which are already in the news lately following the recent tragic death of businessman Manish Shah."

"Cut," shouts Amar, who is tall, lanky and kind of a boy-next-door. He admiringly notes, "Zoya, *tujhe toh* actress *banna chahiye*. Bollywood's number one heroine!"

Jimmy, who is a few inches shorter but has a model's good looks and a gym-toned eight-pack abs, cuts him short, saying, "Amar, *bas kar*. You can sing Zoya's praises later. For now, let's decide where to start."

Amar looks in the direction of the horsemen, who are standing by the entrance of the station, and eagerly waits for them to draw closer. Zoya immediately shakes her head. "No, they will be wary after that accident two days ago; they won't say much. Let's proceed on foot in the direction of the stables. There are some down there." She points to a road going downhill. "Those working there will be more forthcoming."

Amar looks at her with wide-eyed admiration. "You are so smart, Zoya, but how do you know there are stables there? Like us, this is your first trip to Matheran."

She ignores him and keeps her eyes firmly on Jimmy, who is walking ahead and filming the narrow trails as the surrounding mountains rise steeply on one side and fall sharply on the other. He takes 360-degree shots of the impressive panoramic view. While Zoya's eyes keenly follow Jimmy, those of Amar are transfixed on her. Priya runs alongside the three, cutting through the crackling sexual tension in the air. Shortly after, Zoya spots a stable and waves to her companions. As they near it, Rashid steps out, looking disturbed. Zoya steps into his path, all beguiling charm. "Hello, I'm Zoya and these are my friends. A couple of days ago, Manish Shah, a businessman from Mumbai, fell from his horse and died. Can you tell us something about that accident?"

Rashid eyes her suspiciously. There is something about her which is familiar. Has he seen her before in Matheran, he wonders, his brow furrowing. His eyes narrow as he notices

Amar pointing his camera at him and snaps, "Why do you want to know? Are you presswallahs? I have nothing more to say. I have said all that I could to the policewallahs and presswallahs. Again and again and again."

Zoya shakes her head and assures the exasperated ghodawallah that they have nothing to do with the fourth estate or the cops. "We are from Mumbai and heard about the accident on the way here. I was only checking to see if riding in Matheran is still safe?"

It suddenly dawns on Rashid that the accident could make tourists like them apprehensive and rob the horsemen of their livelihood again. Instantly, he gives her a reassuring smile. "*Arre nahi,* madam-ji. There's no need to be afraid. *Bilkul* safe *hai*. I'll take all of you to Sunset Point myself if you want."

She flashes him another smile and tells him that they will take him up on the offer the next day. "For now, we have to find a lodge that fits our minuscule budget," she says.

Rashid is looking around, as if searching for someone. He mumbles, "Bingo has been missing for three days now. God alone knows where he is."

Zoya gently prods, "Who's Bingo? Your brother?"

Rashid shakes his head dolefully. "He's our horse." His face crumples and his eyes moisten as he desperately tries to hold back his tears. Things are falling apart at home. His father is beginning to lose hope of ever finding Bingo and has been drinking heavily. Last night, he hit their mother, and this morning, Abbu picked up a fight with his elder brother, Arshad. Will he turn into another Suresh bhai?

Zoya and Jimmy exchange glances as they look at the distraught boy, who is around their age, and instinctively gather that there is a story here. Jimmy wisely decides to leave the talking to Zoya. She questions Rashid in a way that doesn't raise his hackles, and Jimmy has to agree with Amar that the girl is a born journalist and actress. But he will never admit this publicly.

Zoya already has a swollen head, thinks Jimmy. He doesn't want her to feel even more self-important. He prefers girls like Priya, who do not put on airs. He knows it rankles Zoya that he would choose plain, simple Priya over her. He doesn't feel the need to explain. He tunes back into the conversation.

Rashid is telling Zoya that they haven't seen the horse since the accident. "But a couple of people have spotted him from afar. They say he's like a phantom horse now. Usmein bhoot bas gaya hai," he wails.

Jimmy can't believe what he's hearing. These people live on another planet, he silently mutters to himself. "Superstition, gossip and hearsay thrive here—undoubtedly the result of poverty and illiteracy!" While he prudently stays silent, Priya bursts out laughing, telling Rashid there is no such thing as a horse possessed by a ghost. Haunted mansions maybe but not horses!

Zoya rounds on her angrily, hissing at her to shut her "bloody mouth". Turning back to Rashid, she placatingly says, "I believe you." But the mood is broken. In the face of Priya's open scepticism and the two boys' curious stares, Rashid clams up.

Knowing she will not get anything more from Rashid, Zoya turns to the camera that Amar has thankfully kept whirring and begins to speak in English so that the ghodawallah will not understand her. With an amused glint in her eyes, she says, "Guys, did you hear that? For the first time ever, we have just heard of a horse being possessed. Amazing, right?"

She then walks away from the range of the camera and turns back to Rashid. "I want to see your Bingo. *Kahan dikhai dega woh*?" He laughs dryly, stating that she will see many a Bingo in Matheran, for it's a common horse name. "But our

Bingo is big, black and beautiful—a stallion that is the star of our stables. Every tourist wants to ride him. We could never have afforded a horse like him if the Iranis had not…" He stops upon being interrupted by his father, who is calling out to him from the direction of the station and telling him that the next train will arrive in five minutes.

Rashid shouts out that he's on the way and hurriedly turns to Zoya, saying, "*Dhandhe ka* time *hai*, madam-ji. I have to earn a living or I will get a good hiding from Abbu. *Baad mein fursat se baat karte hain*. Are you in Matheran for some time?"

Zoya nods. "Yes, we are here for a couple of days."

He tells her that he will catch up with her soon and runs off. She calls out to him, asking him where they can spot Bingo, but he doesn't look back. Either he hasn't heard or chooses not to answer.

She waits till he is out of earshot before turning back to the camera. "So, guys, as you can see, we have barely reached Matheran and already we have learnt about a haunted horse. Keep logging in and I will keep blogging. Back with more spooky tales soon. For now, I have to go look for Bingo."

She signs off with a two-finger bye and tells her friends that she knows of a lodge that is clean and cheap. "It's just a little way down from Garbett Point. No one goes there except for an occasional foreigner. Follow me."

This time Amar voices his surprise. "How come you know so much about Matheran? Have you been here before?"

She laughs gaily. "Yeah, in another life." She laughs harder at the expression on his face and taps on her phone, saying, "*Buddhu*, Google *hai na*?! I did a little web surfing on our way, and now I know as much as the locals do."

She suddenly realises that her throat is parched. Spotting a shack across the road, she runs across to buy a bottle of water.

As the shopkeeper is counting the change, something catches her eye. It's the statue of a black horse, with its front legs raised. As she gazes at it, the eyes suddenly come alive. In them, she sees the reflection of another horse—big, black and beautiful. On its yellow saddle, his name is inscribed: Bingo. She hears a galloping sound and looks over her shoulder. There is no horse, but Amar jumps on her, making her start.

She screams and he hoots. "Our Zoya is a *fattu! Bhoot pret ki kahani sun ke darr gayi hai*. Hey baby, what are you afraid of? A possessed horse coming along?"

With a trembling finger, Zoya points to the road and says, "I saw him. I saw Bingo. I saw him in the other horse's eyes." She turns to look at the statue of the horse, whose eyes are stony and opaque again.

Amar shouts out to the others, exclaiming, "Hey, guys, come here! Our Zoya is well and truly spooked. She is beginning to see phantom horses now."

Priya runs up and reprimands him. "Amar, stop teasing Zoya." She notices with concern that the other girl is looking unnaturally pale and says, "I think we need to find a place to crash and get something to eat asap. It's been a long wait for breakfast."

She reaches for Zoya's hand. It is deathly cold. Her eyes are still fixed on the statue. Priya tugs on her hand gently, saying, "Come along, Zoya. Let's go and find a place to stay."

The other girl turns to her and whispers, "I saw the horse. And I saw *her*."

Priya nods, soothingly saying, "I'm sure you did. Now, come along."

For once, Zoya doesn't protest, letting Priya lead her away. As the four youngsters head off, the statue of the horse watches them go, its eyes alive and glittering again.

12

The Secret Warehouse

In the dining hall of Cecil Lodge, Sara, Sana and Sid are having breakfast. Madhu has served them cereal, milk and toast. He is now in the kitchen and stirring up some scrambled eggs. The twins look at the portraits of the Parsis around them, who seem intimidating. Trying not to be scared of these forbidding figures, the two decide to give them funny names.

Sara points to a picture of an elderly gentleman in traditional attire and headgear, flanked by his wife and two sons and their wives. She giggles and says, "That's Dadabhai Navroze with his *pariwar*."

Sid instantly shakes his head and, spooning cornflakes into his mouth, mumbles, "No, that's Daruwalla Dadu."

His cousin frowns her displeasure. "So, you are back to playing your games, huh? Let me tell you it's not funny." She is interrupted by her sister, who is peering at the name beneath the picture. Surprised, Sana says, "He's right, Sara. The man's name is Persi Daruwalla, and those are his two sons, Cyrus and Behram. The names of the ladies are not written though."

Sid obviously knows them well because pat comes the answer: "That one there is Deena Dadi," he says, pointing to the elderly lady. Gesturing to the two younger ones, he adds, "And that's Dolly Aunty and Kainaz Aunty. The aunties and Dadi were nice, but Dadu was very set in his ways and thinking and took them away. How much they cried when they were leaving, begging him to change his mind, but he wouldn't listen."

While Sana gapes at him, wide-eyed, Sara is determined to call his bluff. "And who is that man there?" she says, pointing to another portrait.

Sid doesn't even pause to think, "That's Dadu's friend, Maneckji Shapurji Sarabji." The name is a mouthful, but he doesn't stumble.

Sana points to a lady in a sari and giggles. "And who's she, Siddie?"

The little boy identifies her as Mehr Aunty and the man in the photograph next to hers as Phiroz Uncle. "They too went away to build a fortune in America."

Sara is still sceptical, unimpressed by the abbreviated family histories Sid is appendaging the portraits with. He is unconcerned and continues with his monologue as he says, "That's Rustom bhai—he loved to play football. Sanaya Aunty made the best *mithoo dahi* and yummy *malai na khaja*." He licks his lips but begins to frown as he turns to the man in the next picture. "Sam Uncle there was mean and Sohrab Nana had the worst temper. But Zarine Jiji told such lovely stories."

While these people are complete strangers to the girls, they seem to be Sid's family and community in his narration, as though he has grown up among them. Madhu enters the dining room with eggs just as Sid turns to look at a picture of a lady with a little boy of his age sitting on her lap. He knows them better than the rest and smiles as he announces, "And that's Parzaan and Shahnaz Mamma."

The helper almost drops the platter in shock even as Sana says, "Yes, you introduced us to them last night at dinner. And Parzaan…Didn't I hear you say that name this morning at Sunrise Point when you were insisting on returning home and playing with him. Does he live around the lodge?"

Sid nods. "He lives here."

Sana is instantly excited. "Oh good! Then we can all play together. It is a little lonely here without our friends."

Sid shakes his head. "I don't know if he will play with you."

Sara snaps, "Yeah, how can he? He's a figment of your imagination."

Standing behind them and holding the platter in a death grip, Madhu whispers, "No, he isn't."

The girls don't hear him, but Sid looks directly at the helper with a strange smile.

***

In the bungalow, Kiara is pointing to a pile of stuff that she has dumped in the corner of their bedroom. There are clothes, sheets of expired pills, some old toys and other riff raffs. "I want you to dispose of all this," she tells Aditya.

He is mesmerised. His wife has never looked so sexy, so desirable. It's the dress—he's never seen it before. She must have bought it recently. And the perfume that has his senses swimming—that's new too.

He wraps his arms around her. For a minute Kiara freezes. Gently, he turns her towards him and starts pulling down the dress, all the while nibbling on her earlobes, dropping soft kisses along her jaw and nuzzling the pulse in her throat.

Kiara's moans stir Aditya further as his lips lock on hers before whispering, "This lipstick. It's so hot! My blood is boiling."

She laughs, tossing her curls, and he sighs, "And your hair! It's different too. You are different today somehow. I want you, baby. I need you."

She laughs throatily. "Didn't you get enough of me last night that you want me for breakfast now? The kids will be wondering where we have disappeared."

Aditya, nipping on her lips, says, "Chill. They are having breakfast. Madhu's there with them. They won't miss us."

At the sound of Madhu's name, Kiara stiffens again, but Aditya is too aroused to notice. "Come on, baby. Something inside me is turning wild for you. Don't shut me off now. I will die."

Kiara laughs and draws him towards the bed. He doesn't resist, putty in her wandering hands. With one hard shove, she has him spread-eagled on the bed, and in a swift move that takes him by surprise, she mounts him. She is the aggressor and knows exactly what she wants. He doesn't complain. Soon, their cries reverberate around the room. Kaira pants in the throes of passion and Aditya groans as she drives him crazy. "Faster…Faster…Oh my God! Don't stop now. Please no."

Kiara laughs and throws her head back, looking at the ceiling. And in that moment, she changes. It's not Kaira making love to Aditya—it's Shahnaz.

Aditya's eyes are closed; he is in heaven. His wife has never taken him like this. She is an animal in bed today, and he doesn't mind despite the painful scratches. Her nails are like talons, drawing blood. He wonders when she grew them. Kiara has never liked long nails. Maybe they are artificial ones which she has fixed on. They are super sexy. And her eyes are pitch black. She must be wearing lenses, he concludes.

***

In the lodge, the kids are playing blind man's buff. Blindfolding Sid and asking him to count till ten before starting his search, the girls run off giggling as they look for a good hiding place. They run down the corridor, peeping into rooms, and continue running till they come to a door that is shut. While Sana stands stock-still looking at it, Sara moves forward and turns the knob. It's the library. Dark inside and funny-smelling, but it is a good hiding place. She can hear Sid approaching them and pulls Sana into the room and behind a book stand as he calls out to them.

Sara looks around and whispers, "Lots of books and more pictures. He's going to see them and start coming up with more names and stories." Sana laughs.

The door opens and Sid stands framed in a strange bluish light.

***

Aditya, freshly showered and dressed, looks satiated as he steps out of the villa and moves towards the garbage dump with the stuff Kiara has asked him to dispose of. He throws them and turns, watching his wife walk towards him. A frown beetles his brow.

She's different again—more like the Kiara he is used to. If anyone were to ask him how he knows, he wouldn't know what to say. He just knows deep down. She's sweet rather than brazenly sexy. But her soft hazel eyes forever remind him that she is the woman he gave his whole heart to over a decade ago. Even though the other one was exciting and a tigress in bed, he prefers this Kiara. He waits till she catches up with him and then, reaching for her hand, entwines her fingers with his.

They walk companionably towards the lodge, hand in hand, with Aditya saying, "I hope breakfast is ready. I'm starving.

Thanks to you, I am building up quite an appetite here and not just for food." Kiara blushes and stays silent.

Madhu watches them from a distance. As soon as they disappear into the lodge, he rushes to the dustbin and starts going through the stuff Aditya has dumped. He gathers up the clothes, a discarded bottle of perfume, a hair brush with strands of hair still entwined in it and a torn stuffed toy Joker with a painted smile. Clutching them, he runs off in the direction of the woods.

Inside the house, there's a loud thud and the sound of a child crying out. Kiara and Aditya, who are sedately strolling down the corridor towards the dining room, race towards the sound upon hearing it and anxiously call out to the kids. Sara hollers from inside the library and Aditya bursts in, immediately noticing the twins and Sid clustered around the bookcase which has fallen. It's obvious from his face that his son is the culprit.

He rebukes him sharply. "Sid, I know this is your doing. Do you realise you could have got hurt? There's a lot of old stuff around this place which is expensive and delicate. You all need to be careful. Sara and Sana, Sid is a brat, but you are older and should have known better than to…"

Sana looks at him guilty. "We were hiding behind it and Sid…"

Sid interrupts her. "I didn't do anything, Papa. I swear I didn't. I just yanked the handle and the case fell down. I didn't do anything."

Kiara points to a dark space in the wall and nudges Aditya. "Look…" Peering, he notices a trapdoor in the wall and pushes it. It swings open. The girls push forward and gasp as they see the opening. Sid tries to muscle his way to the front, but Aditya pushes them back, telling Kiara to take them to the bathroom so that they can wash the dirt off their hands and faces.

"I will check this out," he says, reaching inside and fumbling for a switch. He finds one and flicks it, yelping as current shoots through him. However, a lone bulb flickers to life. In the dim light, he can see a stairway festooned with cobwebs, going up.

"Is this the way to hidden treasures?" Sara asks excitedly, leaning over his shoulder.

Aditya slants her a wry grin. "I doubt it. But I am going to go up and check."

Kiara looks him straight in the eye and decisively says, "And we are going to wait right here till you get back."

Aditya would argue, but he knows from the mulish expression on his wife's face that she will not change her mind. So he nods obligingly. "Okay, but make sure these brats don't follow me. We have no idea what's up there and from the look of things, it's filthy and hasn't been cleaned in months."

Picking up a fallen book, he waves at the cobwebs. They tear, making his passage easier. He walks up a dozen steps and reaches the attic. Actually, it's more like a warehouse—a 2000-sq-foot warehouse. "Woah!" he exclaims, stepping inside.

The place is a mess and it smells really bad. It's not just the mildew, but there's something foul in the air here. Holding his breath and pinching his nose with his thumb and forefinger, Aditya moves towards a small window at the far end, flinging it open. There is a rustle of wings as some bats nestling in the room swoop low over his head and fly out. He yelps and goes down on his hunches, their webbed wings brushing his head. Some much-needed fresh air flows into the room, but the stench almost makes him retch. It's eerie and scary here!

Kiara's voice comes up from below. "Hey, what's up there, Aditya? You have been so quiet. Should I come?"

Alarmed, he shouts back, "No, no, don't. I'm coming down."

He stumbles down the stairs and, with a feeling of relief, steps out into the library. He flicks off the light and slams the door shut. "What..." Kiara begins to say but he shakes his head, cuts her short and heads towards the washroom, gagging. It's as if the smell is clinging to his clothes and his skin. Kiara and the kids run after him.

After their exit from the library, the bulb suddenly flickers and lights up on its own. This time it is bright, its light illuminating the warehouse. It is even dirtier than Aditya imagined. The window he had opened suddenly slams shut, and almost in sync, the light goes out. The space is dark and eerie again. The stench is unbearable! Madhu is looking at the house from afar, his eyes fixed on the warehouse. He has seen the light go on, with the shadow of a person moving around it. He sees a window opening and bats flying out. He stares fixedly, watching the person retreat. The light goes off. And comes back on again. He continues to watch with bated breath. He can see a shadow pacing through the room. When the light finally goes off and the window bangs shut, he starts breathing again, walking with leaden steps towards the house.

13

Death in the Valley...Again!

The sky is overcast and the weather dark and gloomy with a hint of rain, as if the air is grieving with the small group gathered at the burial ground to bid adieu to one of their own. As the maulvi says a prayer for the dead man, the coffin is slowly lowered to the ground and the mourners throw handfuls of soil into the freshly dug grave. The two cops stand at a distance watching the proceedings. Tembe looks dazed, like he is in shock, while the inspector is sombre, all traces of the holiday revelry wiped out by the recent tragedy.

Once the funeral is over, the locals turn to head home. Todkar locks eyes with Khan who is in the crowd and, with a barely perceptible nod, beckons him over. For a moment, the elderly man just looks at him without expression and then slowly strolls over.

"*Assalamu alaikum*, Khan sahab," Todkar greets him with a raised palm and a slight bow. The other man reciprocates wordlessly as the inspector sympathetically adds, "I'm sorry for your loss. You must have been close to Abdul."

Khan nods, his eyes shimmering with unshed tears and his voice barely a whisper. "He was like a son to me. In a place this small, everyone's family. We would meet for Friday namaz and he would drop by my lodge often. Abdul loved to eat and before his chachi—my wife—fell ill, she would cook kebabs, *sevaiyan*, and *sheera* for him." His voice cracks as he is suddenly overcome with emotion. "*Kyun*, sahab? Why did this have to happen to the boy? He was so young. Too young to die."

Todkar reaches out and embraces him with empathy. "I can understand how you are feeling. It was a terrible, terrible accident. I still can't believe he is gone."

Khan breaks away from his arms and abruptly asks, "Why was he going up to Garbett, sahab? All of us know better than to go up that way."

The inspector doesn't answer, remembering guiltily that he was the one who had insisted on going up that hill. Abdul had tried to stop him, but he had been deaf to the boy's pleas. Who would have thought...

Khan is looking at him and when he doesn't reply, he raises another query. "Did you see Abdul die? How did it happen?"

Todkar remains silent. He had reached the closed sign and tried to go below the board. Abdul had grabbed him. He had shoved him aside. The last thing he recalls is the boy screaming, "No, sahab, don't go that way. That's where *she* shot..."

The next moment, Abdul was gone, as if pushed by an unseen hand. The boy had gone hurtling down the hill, his head hitting the boulders on the way and his body being pulled down ferociously and mercilessly. He had tumbled to a stop at the junction, almost at the feet of Tembe who had been too frightened to accompany them up.

Todkar had reached the bottom of the hill five minutes later, gasping and winded, only to find the constable staring down at the boy with a dazed and shocked look. Inches away, when he had called out to him, Tembe had looked up and replied in a tremulous voice. "*Mar gaya*, sahib."

Khan is now looking at him. When Tembe also doesn't speak, the old man murmurs, almost to himself, "Destiny—how can we escape it? Or *her*? *Inna lillahi wa inna iluyhi Adityai'un*. I wonder when my turn will come."

He takes a few steps forward towards the gate of the *kabristan* before returning to where the inspector is waiting for him. "You must leave soon, sahab. *Mausam kharab hone laga hai.* It is no longer safe here. Go back. Go back from where you came before it is too late," he says urgently. Then, with a quiet "*Khuda Hafiz*", he hurries away.

Tembe turns to Todkar as he suddenly looks terrified. "What did he mean that it's no longer safe here? Sahib, *kya bol raha tha woh?*" He clutches Todkar's arm and almost shakes him.

The inspector doesn't say a word and simply disengages his clutching fingers and follows Khan out. Tembe stands still in the suddenly deserted graveyard before almost running after Todkar, shouting, "Sahib, wait. Don't leave me alone here. I'm scared."

***

In the bungalow, an excited Aditya tells Kiara that he will be out all day. "Sunny and his team of architects are driving down from Mumbai. I'm meeting them at the hotel where they are staying for the day. I want to convert the warehouse Sid discovered in the lodge into a gaming parlour for kids. Sunny has some ideas and I will be looking over their plans. If I like them, they will start work at the lodge next week. There's lots to be done," he says with a sigh.

The next moment though, Aditya brightens up, saying that once it's all spruced up and the warehouse remodelled, Cecil will be back in business and how! "I've been to all the lodges here. Some of them are indeed good. But they don't have a history like Cecil's and none of them have a gaming room. That will be our big draw. Mark my words," he asserts.

His wife looks unhappy. "Do you really need to go? And can't we just leave that space alone? You did say it was not in the blueprint so maybe it doesn't want to be discovered," she opines.

Aditya turns to her with an amazed expression on his face. "Baby, what are you saying? We just won a lottery and you are asking me to return the money? What's wrong with you?"

She doesn't want to dwell on her apprehensions, which have no reasonable basis, and drops the subject, nervously rubbing her suddenly cold and sweaty palms and asking why the architects can't come there to meet Aditya. "Why do you have to go there? It's a long walk and we will be all alone here," she complains.

Her husband holds her close and kisses her gently. "Don't worry. I'm sure at the junction to Garbett and Sunset Point, I will find a ghodawallah to take me to Mall Road. Perhaps I will run into Suresh bhai. I tried his phone, but as usual, I couldn't get through. Yes, you will be alone all day, but we could do with the occasional breaks, or else we will soon get on each other's nerves. I promise to be back before sundown. You make sure Sid is not up to any mischief."

Aditya hunkers down in front of their son who is gripping his new favourite toy, the bicycle handle, and preparing to vroom off. "Siddie, will you promise Papa that you will be a good boy and not trouble Mamma?"

His son nods obligingly, saying he will play with Parzaan. Aditya rolls his eyes and looks at the twins. Sana tells him reassuringly that they will not let him out of their sight. "Good girl. I'll see you all in the evening then. You have the whole day to explore; maybe you will find me another warehouse! Bye," he says gaily.

A chorus of goodbyes follows him as he walks across the campus and out of the gate. He immediately notices Madhu walking up ahead, holding a hen in his hands that is flapping around and trying to escape. The helper's hands are closed around its scrawny neck. It clucks loudly but Madhu walks on chanting a mantra, seemingly oblivious to his surroundings.

Aditya watches him wide-eyed, wondering what the man is up to. After a dozen circles, Madhu puts the hen into the large cloth bag that he is carrying. It flutters and clucks inside. Aditya follows, making sure to keep a discreet distance between them, though the helper seems to be in a trance.

Madhu suddenly ducks into a thicket by the side of the road. Aditya hears the bird raising a racket. Even as he is wondering what Madhu is doing, the helper steps out, still dazed, without the bag or the hen which is silent now. He starts walking towards the lodge.

It's too late to hide so Aditya does the next best thing. He keeps walking towards Madhu, pretending he hasn't seen anything. The helper's eyes are darting around furtively, guilt written all over his face. Aditya waits till they are within handshaking distance before stepping into his way and asking, "Arre, Madhu, I thought you were at the lodge. Where are you coming from?"

Avoiding his eyes, the other man mumbles, "*Pet mein dard tha*, so I went to get some medicines."

The lie is so blatant that Aditya almost blurts out, "Of course, your stomach will hurt if you fib so much." But biting his tongue, he solicitously says, "I'm sorry to hear that you are not feeling well. I'm going to Mall Road. If you need me to pick up any medicines for you from the chemist there, just give me a call. I will bring them on my way home."

Madhu nods his thanks and replies shortly and a trifle rudely. "I'm fine, my baba told me what to do."

Aditya almost says, "Yeah, I know of your cures," but instead responds, "Okay, take care. *Shaam ko milte hain.*"

At the gate, Madhu turns and watches his employer with anger in his eyes, "Why can't he understand the danger he has put his family in by bringing them here? And now he leaves them alone and goes gallivanting. When will he learn?"

Meanwhile, Aditya is wondering about Madhu. The guy appears to be a weirdo and he doesn't have a good feeling about him. He wishes Shivaji would get back soon so that he can get rid of him. But the caretaker has just disappeared. And till he returns, Aditya doesn't want to sack Madhu, given that the locals seem to be averse to Cecil for some reason. One of these days, he will have to get Suresh to tell him what is keeping them away. But today, he has to decide how best to put the warehouse to use.

He reaches the thicket where Madhu disappeared. He looks behind his shoulder. There is no sign of the helper. Taking a deep breath, Aditya ducks behind the bushes. It's dark and it takes a minute for his eyes to adjust to the loss of the bright sunlight. A few moments later, he sees something that makes him break out in a cold sweat. The hen is dead and lying on the ground with a broken neck. The cloth bag is lying at a distance. Aditya picks it up and rummages through it. He almost screams as he draws out another dead bird.

***

Zoya and her gang are at the junction of Garbett Point and Sunrise Point. The girl is her usual cocky and chirpy self, smiling invitingly into the camera. "Okay, guys. Are you ready for another adventure? Come along then but don't blame me if what happens next scares the daylights out of you!"

She points to the hill. "This is the road leading to Garbett Point. *Haan yeh wohi rasta hai* where recently two deaths have taken place. First, the businessman from Mumbai, Manish Shah, and yesterday, a ghodawallah fell to his death from up there. At this rate, Garbett will quickly become one of the most haunted places in Matheran."

She holds up her hands gleefully. "Well, I'm on my way up there now with my ghostbuster gang—Jimmy, Priya and Amar. And you can join us virtually."

As Amar trails Zoya, Priya drags her feet. Jimmy turns to find her still standing at the junction, looking up at the hill apprehensively. He gently asks, "Priya, what's wrong?"

She says, uncertainly, "Jimmy, do we need to go up there? I'm not getting a good feeling."

Zoya, who has turned to see what's keeping them, teasingly says, "Hey Priya, don't be such a *fattu*. *Chal upar aa*. I promise there are no ghosts here."

Priya shakes her head. "How do you know that? No way am I going up there." Zoya looks irritated now. "You are a sissy. Well stay there if you want, but we are going up. We have a show to bring to our followers. Come along, Jimmy. I'm told the view from up there is awesome."

Priya grabs Jimmy's hand tightly. "He's not going up. And neither are Amar and you. Please come down. Something doesn't feel right."

Zoya opens her mouth to refute her when Jimmy placatingly says, "Let's avoid Garbett for now, Zoya. The road is closed anyway. Let's go to Sunrise Point instead."

While Priya looks relieved, the other girl scowls, pointing out that the sun has already risen. Fearing a tantrum, Amar turns the camera towards himself and speaks into it. "Sorry guys, the way up is closed. So, we have to put off this visit for another day."

As Zoya opens her mouth to argue, Jimmy calls out, "Come along now. Let's not spoil this trip with constant fights. Let's go enjoy the view. Tomorrow we will do as you say."

Somewhat mollified, Zoya nods and retraces her steps to where they are waiting, with Amar following her. Priya shivers, so Jimmy draws her close. Seeing this, Zoya grits her teeth as red hot jealousy courses through her.

14

The Birthday Party

In a café, Aditya is poring over the blueprint of the lodge, pointing out the dining room, the smoker's lounge, the many bedrooms and washrooms, the kitchen and, finally, the library to his team of architects. He then points to a space over the library and exults, "And that's where the warehouse is. It's not marked in the blueprint, but I've been up there and seen it for myself. It's huge—all 2,000 square feet of it!"

Sunny is frowning, wondering why no one knew about it till Sid stumbled and revealed the entrance to it. Aditya admits he has been thinking the same thing. "But because they didn't know about it, I hit a jackpot," he beams.

He tells them excitedly that once they have cleaned it up and got rid of the stench, it will make a perfect play zone. They can have a reading corner and install a train set up as they definitely need some playstations. "The idea is to keep the kids occupied and give parents some much-needed time together. It's thanks to *Jurassic Park Evolution 2*, *Battlefield 2042* and *Call of Duty: Vanguard* that I get my wife to myself occasionally, else Sid is a hard-to-beat rival in love," he confides.

Sunny laughs. "And I'm sure you put that time to good use."

Aditya remembers the rough tumble in the bedroom and is instantly aroused. "Well, it's got plenty hot and heavy since we moved to Matheran," he responds, grinning back.

***

In his bedroom in the villa, Sid is gaming, with his eyes glued to the screen and his fingers dancing over the console. As guns go off and missiles explode, the game reaches fever pitch. The noise is deafening and Sara screams from the other bedroom. "Sid, lower the volume. I can't even hear myself, forget Sana and the songs I'm playing."

Sid ignores her, intent only on destruction. Kiara enters his room with a glass of juice, takes stock of the situation with a sweeping glance and lowers the game's volume. Sid pounces on her aggressively, his hands in a fist. "Why did you do that, Mamma? I'm on the battlefield."

Kiara has to fight to keep her calm. "Sid, behave yourself. How many times have I told you that you are not living here alone? Your cousins are in the next room and you need to be considerate towards them. Ever since we got to Matheran, you have become a brat."

Her son sulks, "But Parzaan..." Kiara waves her hand dismissively, saying that living alone has spoiled Parzaan too and that he also must learn to play more quietly. "And the next time he is in the house or on the grounds, tell him to meet me. I want to see who your little pal is," she says sternly.

From the doorway, the other little boy watches her. She doesn't see him, but Sid does and giggles, making his mother look sharply at him. After making sure that Sid has finished his juice, Kiara sails out of the room and walks downstairs.

Ignoring the gently swaying rocking chair that she has now got used to, she steps out on the porch, her mind on Aditya as she hopes that he will be back before sundown. She tries to shake off the feeling of dread which has enveloped her. "Old houses are lovely, but they are full of secrets, like the warehouse which was sealed off and forgotten. Why? There has to be a reason," she says to herself.

She looks in the direction of the lodge and murmurs, "As I keep telling Aditya, we should let sleeping dogs lie and not wake them up from the dead."

In his bedroom, the frenetic pace of the game is making Sid laugh nervously as he works the console. He is sitting at the edge of his bed as the battle royale heads towards its climax. Parzaan has disappeared. Sid is disappointed by his lack of interest in gaming. It's as if he has never played video games in his life. He's the outdoor type—he likes football, swings and seesaws and just running around the campus.

Suddenly, the electricity goes off. The screen turns black, the fan stops whirring, and even the sunlight seems to have been blotted out. Sid sits back wondering when the power will be back. Next door, Sara and Sana have started complaining loudly. He is about to get up and join them when the screen suddenly flickers to life with images of a birthday party—Parzaan's birthday

There are very few people in the dining room. None from the portraits except Irani Dadu. There is a magic show and a puppet show. Everyone smiles and claps. Parzaan loves the puppets and grabs for a ragtag Joker. The puppeteer tells his mother that he can have it on his special day.

As Sid watches wide-eyed, the boy's mother, Shahnaz, walks up with a large cake and sets it on the table in the lodge's dining room. She lights the candle. It's numbered one. They begin singing the 'Happy Birthday' song.

Shahnaz blows out the candles with one puff and cuts the cake. She feeds Parzaan a bite and hands the rest around. As everyone nibbles on a slice, Dadu hands the birthday boy a gift wrapped in glittering paper.

His mother rips off the wrapping to reveal a big red football. Sid responds to the 'surprise' with the same delighted smile as Parzaan's and the screen blanks out again, but the fan starts whirring. There are loud whoops from the next room. The electricity has returned, but his game screen remains dead.

Even as Sid is wondering if he should call his mother, with a thump, thump, thump, the football he has just seen rolls into the room, coming to a stop near his feet. He looks down at it, mesmerised. He picks it up and looks towards the door. Parzaan is standing there, beckoning him.

As their eyes meet, the other boy turns about and runs. Sid jumps up and, holding the football to his chest, chases after him, shouting, "Parzaan, wait! I'm coming to play with you." As two pairs of legs, only one of them visible, go thudding down the stairs, the girls look at each other. Sara shrugs disdainfully. "Sid has been behaving really strangely since we got here. He seems to have found himself a whole new family and a bestie none of us can see. Soon he won't want to have anything to do with us."

Sana, who is watching her young cousin from the window as he runs across the campus yelling out to "Parzan", whispers, "Something is very wrong here. I'm scared."

***

Kiara is standing outside the villa, fiddling with her phone. "Damn, this place sucks! I don't know where to find the network. I really need to call Didi and Jiju to tell them what's going on here. Aditya is deaf to all reason, but this place is beginning to spook me."

As she waits for the network, she clicks some pictures of the property with her cellphone camera. She then twirls and smiles for the photos before bending her head to check the selfies.

***

Inside the lodge, Sid is racing down the corridor, chasing after Parzaan who is a blurry figure ahead of him. As Sid screams at him to stop, he turns to look at him over his shoulder but doesn't stop running. However, he drops the toy he is carrying. It is the ragtag Joker Aditya had dumped in the garbage. Sid picks it up and runs to catch up with Parzaan.

***

Kiara is smiling over the selfies she has just taken, scrolling through the photo gallery to select her best profile shots and give them filter effects. In one of the pictures, she notices a woman standing at the window of one of the rooms of the lodge as she watches her. The image is out of focus, but the woman is clearly visible. The phone drops from Kiara's numb fingers.

She turns to look at the same window. There is no one there now. A chill courses through her. Shivering, she bends down to pick up the phone. She scrolls through the rest of the pictures, checking them minutely. There's nothing there. They are all normal. She returns to the photograph of the woman. She sees only the window—there is no one looking out.

Kiara turns to walk back to the bungalow. Instinct makes her look up. Sid is sitting on the parapet of the lodge's terrace, his legs dangling as he smiles at her. She opens her mouth to scream, but no sound comes out. Even as she watches, a woman walks up and stands right behind Sid. With one gentle shove, she can send him tumbling down to the ground. Kiara screams, "Sid, no! Get back, baby."

Her son doesn't move. She can still see the woman behind him and makes a dash for the house. She flies up the stairs, panting, and runs up to the roof. Sid's back is visible to her, but there is no sign of anyone else. Softly, so as not to startle him, Kiara walks up to stand behind him in the exact place where the other woman was standing moments earlier.

Taking a deep breath, she reaches for Sid. He doesn't resist as she gently pulls him towards her. It's almost like he was expecting her. She lifts him up and cradles him to her chest, sobbing. He gently strokes her hair and, still smiling, says, "Mamma, don't cry. Parzaan will not say bye bye."

15

Trail of Blood

It is late afternoon and Aditya is walking down Mall Road, having finished his meeting with the architects. It went well and he is excited. Sunny and his team have left for Mumbai to pick up supplies. They will be back in Matheran by the end of the week and will start work immediately. He wants them to move into the lodge so that they won't have to commute after a long day's work. "I have to get Madhu to clean out some of the bedrooms and I hope he will go back to the Parsi cuisine he welcomed us with. His cooking has deteriorated since then and his khichdi and kadi is not going to win him any brownie points with this bunch," he mutters, remembering how Madhu had denied preparing the earlier meal. Insisting that he had never made dhanshak and custard in his life, he had turned ashen upon hearing what had been on the table. Instead, he had blamed Aditya for dumping the food he had cooked in the dustbin that night. As if the family would be so insensitive, Aditya thinks as he rolls his eyes. Who throws food away? They have been having his indifferent meals for days. The man must suffer from a split personality!

Aditya remembers the dead chicken in the thicket, their necks broken, and shivers. "I thought he was getting properly cleaned meat from the market, but obviously he likes playing the butcher himself. Still, it's a strange way to kill the birds. The man is loony."

The scene plays out again in his mind and he whispers, "After what I saw this morning, I doubt if I will be able to dig into the chicken curry prepared by that Madhu again. I wish Shivaji would return. I want to get rid of this *pagal*." Aditya is suddenly aware that he is being watched. Looking ahead, he notices Suresh standing across the street. Immediately, a smile lights up his face at the prospect of going home on one of the ghodawallah's horses.

To his surprise, instead of returning his greeting, Suresh takes off in a hurry in an obvious attempt to avoid him. He is soon lost in the bustling crowd on Mall Road. Ever since the pandemic ended, people have been loath to spend time at home. They are everywhere. Well, who is he to complain! He needs them in Cecil Lodge and can't wait to throw open the doors. If Sunny sticks to the deadline, they will be in business before the year is out. Perhaps they can bring in the New Year with their guests, Kiara on his arm and the kids under their feet. Suresh is nowhere to be seen, but Aditya will not be put off easily. He has to get to the bottom of the horseman's strange behaviour. As the crowd thins, he spots him running into one of the by-lanes. Aditya gives chase.

They race through narrow lanes, over a bridge and into the woods. Suresh slips on the slope and lands on his face. Panting and breathless, Aditya collars him and asks, "What's wrong with you, man? Why are you hiding from me now? Why is everyone in Matheran behaving weirdly?"

Suresh doesn't reply, but from the expression on his face, it is evident that he is rattled. He opens his mouth and the noxious fumes have Aditya recoiling. Wrinkling his nose in disgust, he exclaims, "You are reeking of alcohol! How long have you been drinking?"

With a defeated sigh, Suresh collapses in a heap by the side of the road. "Since *she* died."

***

Zoya and her gang of ghost trackers are at Sunrise Point. Standing at the edge of the iron railing, she cups her hands around her mouth and shouts, "Bingo…Bingo…Bingo." Her voice reverberates around the valley.

Amar guffaws, "Come on, Zoya. *Naam bhi liya to bhootiya ghode ka*!"

Zoya laughs back. "Chill, *yaar*! There's no ghost, no possessed horse, and no hauntings despite all our YouTube claims. These are just urban myths spun by the locals to get tourists to return to Matheran after the pandemic robbed them of their livelihoods. The recent deaths are nothing but accidents and not the work of some vengeful spirit. *Yeh sab to kahaniyon mein hota hai* or in films. None of it is for real."

Priya, who's been silent since they began the climb, shakes her head and asserts that something strange is going on that the local people are keeping to themselves. "I can sense some dark secrets buried here," she whispers.

Zoya eyes her disdainfully and scoffs, "I don't know about the locals, but you have certainly been behaving strangely since we got there—acting like a sissy back there and not letting us go up to Garbett. Now here, too, you are talking about dark secrets. Chill, Priya. Everything's fine, and to prove that, why don't you too shout out to Bingo just like I did. I promise you that that phantom horse is not going to materialise out of thin air and come charging in our direction. Now, do as I say. Come on, you *fattu*!"

Priya is distinctly uncomfortable and looks around for Jimmy. He has wandered off to the other side and is reeling off shots of the valleys. She looks back at Zoya whose eyes are fixed on her, daring her to refuse. Reluctantly, cupping her palms around her mouth, she hollers, "Jimmy…Jimmy…Jimmy…"

As her voice resonates around them, Jimmy swivels and looks at her. Priya offers him a shy smile. He answers with an amused laugh. Tossing her head angrily, Zoya stomps off towards the road taking them down and forces out a laugh. "Come along, guys. The sun is going down and it will soon get dark. I don't want to stumble and tumble and break my crown like Jill. Time to get back and die another day."

Amar, following in her footsteps, teases, "Zoya, what if we meet Bingo on the way? You did call out to him just now."

She shrugs nonchalantly, her mind still on Jimmy and his growing closeness to Priya. "If we do, we can blog about the damn horse," she snaps.

They are halfway down the hill and it's quickly got dark. Zoya's suddenly scared. Sensing it, Amar reaches for her hand and suggests a game of *antakshari* as he thinks this might be his chance to open his heart to her. He's had a crush on her since that first day when he literally bumped into her on the college staircase. Now, he believes, it's more than just an infatuation—he's fallen in love with her. "*Aye mere humsafar, ek zara intezar, sun sadayein de rahi hai manzil pyaar ki…*" he croons, wearing his heart on his sleeve.

Quick on the uptake, Zoya sings back. "*Ab hai judaai ka mausam, do pal ka mehman, kaise na jaayega andhera, kyun na thamega toofan…*" But he protests saying that she needs to think of a new song rather than continuing with his. Looking him straight in the eye, Zoya retorts that she was simply answering him back. Amar falls silent upon realising that it's her way of telling him that she is not interested. He is crushed! It's all because of Jimmy, he admits to himself.

Meanwhile, to grab Jimmy's attention, Zoya asks him what he thinks about paranormal investigators. "They have been trending since Manish Shah's accident. Do you think they are genuine?" she asks.

Jimmy reacts explosively. "I think they are bloody frauds. Their work is gimmicky. I mean how can you track down a spirit with those fancy gadgets!"

Amar, trying to cover his hurt over Zoya's rejection and act like everything is normal, pipes up, "I'm with you on this, Jimmy. These ghost doctors are bullshit!"

"They are the new-age tantric babas," adds Priya.

Zoya snaps her fingers. "Okay. So why don't we blog about them?"

Amar gives her a high five. "That sounds cool."

Jimmy is more guarded in his response, pointing out that they have to be prepared for trolls.

Zoya is unconcerned. "At least we will make a lot of noise and get more followers in the bargain. That's the idea, right?"

Jimmy doesn't dispute her. In the pin-drop silence of their surroundings, the crushing of leaves and the scattering of stones by their feet is the only noise to be heard. Priya fills her lungs with fresh mountain air and sighs contentedly. "This place is almost surreal in its beauty and serenity. I feel so at peace here."

"RIP. Rest in peace," Zoya mutters, making Amar chuckle, even as Jimmy wraps an arm around Priya's shoulders and hums, "*Aati hai to chal mere saath mein, de de saathiyana haathon ko haath mein, rehna hai har pal ab tere saath mein, le le saathiyaa, haathon ko haath mein...*" Stung by his open declaration of love, Zoya rounds on Priya aggressively. "So now this place is beautiful, huh? Where did your ghosts go?"

Before Priya can reply, Jimmy softly says, "Zoya, we've been out all day since yesterday. And I don't have a single footage in my camera that resembles anything remotely haunted."

She reacts by telling Amar commandingly to turn on his camera. He automatically submits to her bidding and she faces it with her usual chutzpah. "Hi guys. I'm back to tell you that we are at the exact same location where Manish Shah fell off his horse and died last week. It's late evening and I'm hoping we can show you a paranormal encounter live. But I have to warn you to not raise your hopes too high because we haven't seen anything out of the ordinary in the last forty-eight hours. And that makes me believe that all these ghost stories about this hill station are but part of an elaborate hoax, being perpetuated by the locals themselves to bring in business. But being ghostbusters and not gimmicky paranormal doctors, we are here to show you that there are no haunted places in Matheran. Absolutely no hauntings. I mean it. NO hauntings."

Listening to her, Priya clutches Jimmy's arm and urgently says, "Make her stop. Please. She is tempting the ghosts."

Before Jimmy can say anything, Zoya adds, "That's the road leading up to Garbett Point. It is said that the horse carrying Manish Shah came hurtling down from up there. And on that side are the supposed haunted railway tracks, and that's the tunnel out of which a train is said to come chugging along. And here is that dark patch the horsemen refuse to ride through. As you can see, everything's fine and perfectly normal. So chill, guys. We have put to rest all the rumours. Goodnight and sweet dreams. Mind you, no nightmares now."

Almost on cue, Amar's camera switches off on its own. "The battery just died, Zoya," he says apologetically.

She is unconcerned. "No stress. We are done for the day. Now, let's get to the hotel asap. I'm starving and I want a good..." Before she can finish the sentence, Jimmy's camera also goes off and so do the street lights. It's pitch dark. Priya can't stifle an involuntary scream.

Jimmy fiddles with his cellphone and tut-tuts, saying, "Girls, stay close to us. The road ahead is bad. Zoya, switch on your mobile torch. My phone is dead!"

She tries but her touch screen is frozen, and Priya's battery is also fully drained. The youngsters can't seem to find any light source. Suddenly spooked, they walk ahead, trying to figure out landmarks from memory.

"Just a few metres ahead, the road to our lodge veers to the right, from where we have to go down the hill. Don't miss the turn," Jimmy instructs.

Everyone nods mutely. The silence is absolute and spine-chilling. The girls huddle together, bonded by their mutual fear. The boys stick close to them and each other, trying to pretend that they are keeping their cool when they are actually shivering in their shoes. Amar is reciting 'Hanuman Chalisa' under his breath. Jimmy hears him but does not comment. Zoya reaches for Priya's hand and jumps. She puts a hand on the other girl's forehead. It's burning. "Priya, you have a fever!" she exclaims. Priya tries to force a laugh, but it comes out as a whimper.

Both boys stop and turn towards her. Jimmy is concerned. "You should have told us you weren't feeling well instead of wandering around in the sun all day with us," he reprimands.

Amar is surprised. "But you were fine up there." He stops as he hears a noise. They all do. A horse is galloping at a distance, with the sound increasing as it draws closer. Amar hopes it is some ghodawallah, but deep down, he knows this is no ordinary horse.

Priya whispers, "It's Bingo!"

Jimmy hears her but pretends he hasn't, urging them to walk faster even as the sound of the horse closes in.

They are all terrified. A slice of moon peeks out, and in its silvery light, the black stallion is clearly outlined. "It's Bingo," Zoya reiterates in a strong and firm voice. Amar pees in his pants and Priya almost swoons. Jimmy catches her before she falls and, grabbing her shoulders, commands, "Run."

Stumbling, the four rush into the darkness as the moon disappears. Bats swoop over their heads and monkeys screech as the sound of thundering hooves gets closer…

***

Aditya is sitting on a stool in Suresh's stable with a glass of tea in his hand. The ghodawallah is sitting opposite him on a bale of hay and his wife, Suman, is standing beside him. For long minutes, everyone is silent. Finally, Aditya says, "Okay, Suresh bhai. Give it to me straight. What the hell is wrong with my property?"

Suresh's eyes are fixed to the floor and he squirms. "Cecil *mein bhoot hai*, baba. That property is haunted."

For a minute, Aditya doesn't react but he soon guffaws. "Did you make me run all this way just to tell me such crap? Had I known, I wouldn't have wasted my stamina."

Suman intervenes, earnestly saying, "*Yeh sach hai*, sahab. *Yeh vaise bewda hai*, but right now he is neither drunk nor lying. *Woh jagah theek nahin hai*. Shahnaz haunts the place. You should leave."

An exasperated Aditya jumps to his feet and, politely thanking Suman for the tea, asks Suresh to come to the lodge the next morning. "I want to take Kiara for a ride. The kids can stay with Madhu," he says.

Suresh pleads with him to heed their warnings, pointing out that he has nothing to gain from spinning a web of lies. "My wife has been urging me to tell you the truth since I took you to the lodge on the day you landed. The broker who sold you the property should have done so, but I guess he just wanted to get rid of the place and you must have paid him good money. *Saala bhaag gaya,*" he admonishes.

Aditya can smell the alcohol on his breath and wonders if the heavy drinking has affected his mind too. The man is still mumbling. "*Sach hai,* baba. *Meri baat mano, yahan se nikal jao.* You are in danger here."

His wife picks up the refrain, insisting that the lodge is haunted, in particular room 19, which was once Shahnaz's bedroom. She goes on to say that there is often a stream of blood in the bathroom drain. Aditya turns towards her, eyes lit up with curiosity. "Oh, so she was murdered? By her own family or intruders?"

Suman shakes her head as her hands fidget. Unwilling to divulge the details, she just says, "The property is haunted, sahab." Her listener, however, is unimpressed and already distracted.

The sun has gone down. Kiara would be getting really anxious, Aditya worries. He needs to get back to his wife and the kids. He wants to take her in his arms and...

He stuffs some money in Suman's hands and tells her to take care. She whispers, "And you take care of your son, sahab. He is not safe in that house." Aditya hears her but doesn't deign to reply as he walks swiftly towards the door.

Suresh calls out after him, saying, "Baba, wait! I will saddle up one of the horses for you. I am coming too. The lodge is far, and you can't walk there in the dark." Finally, Aditya smiles.

But Suman frowns. Her husband is going to Cecil again. He avoids her eyes as he brings out the horses.

***

At the lodge, Madhu has dug a hole in the ground behind the water pump. He gingerly picks up Parzaan's toys, which are wrapped in red, yellow and white threads given to him by the aghori baba, and drops them in the freshly dug hole. Instantly, a boy starts crying behind him. Madhu starts but doesn't look back. If he did, he would see him holding the ragtag Joker.

He picks up the boy's T-shirt and drops that in the pit too. The helper is bare-chested, his body streaked with ashes. Next, he cuts three lemons through the middle and exorcises himself with them. Following this, he throws the pieces in all four directions—north, south, east and west. This time, the cry behind him is louder, almost a protest, and in a woman's voice. It gives him goosebumps!

He covers the freshly dug 'grave' with shovel-fuls of soil. Once it is covered, he lines it with white powdered salt while chanting a mantra. Suddenly, he starts, his eyes swivelling towards the main gate. He has just heard the sound of a horse's hooves and it turns his blood cold. Is it Bingo?

He hurries away. Behind him, a red chiffon scarf flutters and is picked up by the breeze. Madhu doesn't notice.

16

Pool of Deception

As the horse comes into view, Madhu sighs with relief. It's not the wildly galloping stallion Bingo. This horse is chestnut brown and trotting gently. It could be Badal, one of Suresh's horses, though Madhu can't be sure from this distance.

Suresh is accompanying Aditya to the lodge but gets edgy as soon as the property comes into view. The ghodawallah's eyes are darting around fearfully, as if looking for something or someone. Madhu quickly hides behind a tree, not wanting either of the guys to spot him.

Near the gate, Aditya is trying to persuade Suresh to come inside and meet Kiara and the kids. The other man shakes his head vigorously. "No, baba. It's getting dark. I need to get back home. Suman will worry."

Remembering how reluctant she had been to let the horseman escort him to the lodge, Aditya doesn't argue and simply pays him the fare, adding a generous tip. Suresh smiles his thanks, promising to return in the morning.

Minutes later, he disappears down the road with the horses and Aditya makes his way home. Madhu, who has been watching their every move intently, picks up the shovel and walks away in the direction of the woods.

Behind him a scarf flutters—the same flimsy strip of red chiffon. It flies back to the house.

***

The sun has gone down and darkness has embraced the valley. The road is deserted and Suresh, who is riding Baiju and leading Badal by the reins, is beginning to feel uneasy. He wishes he was home now, bickering with his wife and not out in the cold. A sudden gust of wind makes him shiver. The ghodawallah pulls out a small bottle of desi daru from his coat pocket and takes a swig. The alcohol warms him up and bolsters his courage. He tries to hurry along the horses.

The silence is broken by a faint sound. It's a woman humming. It seduces his senses. With his ears strumming, a tipsy Suresh stops and checks over his shoulder. There's no one there, and the singing stops abruptly. He nervously titters, "*Lagta hai aaj jaldi chad gayi hai*. I must be drunk already."

He upends the bottle again while urging Baiju to giddy up. The horse is lethargic. "Suman is right. I pamper you all too much," he grumbles, tightening the reins as the horse falls back again.

The humming starts again—louder this time. Suresh looks to his right. Light is streaming in through the trees. He sees a streak of silver. It takes his sozzled brain a minute or two to comprehend that it's water. Now, he can hear soft and steady splashes.

"Somebody is swimming. But now? In the cold?" he exclaims, rubbing his tired eyes, as he wonders if the cheap alcohol he has got addicted to is short-circuiting his brains. But, no, it's not his inebriated imagination working overtime—there is definitely someone out there.

He gets off the horse, ties both Badal and Baiju to the trees and silently walks down the hill in the direction of the voice. He now remembers that there is a hotel down there, although not very popular with the tourists because it is so far away from the market. Peeping through the trees, he sees that there is at least one guest there now. And she is in the swimming pool.

He watches her pull herself out, shaking off droplets of water clinging to her skin. Her bikini is stringy and she is rather sexy. Suresh is suddenly aroused. He looks down surprised—he had thought that he had lost his libido. For months, he has had no interest in sex, but tonight, he is a man again. As he watches, the woman twists her wet hair into a bun and coils it at the top of her head. It exposes her long, swanlike neck. Suresh imagines nibbling on the tender skin and almost climaxes.

The woman settles into a lounger by the pool, cupping her wine glass. In Suresh's heart, fear has been replaced by a desperate need to see her face…and more. Inching closer, he steps on a dry twig.

The sound is like the crack of a pistol. She jumps up and turns in his direction. He ducks behind the bark of a tree, praying she doesn't spot him. Thankfully, she can't. After a quick scan, she turns her back on him, standing by the pool and sipping her drink as the wet bikini outlines her luscious curves. Then, putting her glass down, she dives in and disappears under water. Suresh sighs as for long minutes he doesn't see her. He is beginning to go crazy with lust.

Her cellphone rings and her head bobs up. Once again, she pulls herself up and, sitting by the edge of the pool, picks up her phone. Almost simultaneously, Suresh's phone rings.

He is shaken as the girl turns in his direction once again. He looks down at the screen—it's a private number. Trembling, he answers it.

"Jaan kab tak wahan se chhip chhip kar mujhe dekhoge? I know you are there. Come closer. I'm waiting for you," she invites in a throaty whisper. He looks up to see her talking into the phone, beckoning him over with a crooked finger.

The moon is out now, but her face is still in the shadows. Trembling, Suresh walks towards the girl whose legs are splashing the water playfully. When he is close, she commands in a voice that brooks no argument and promises a lot. "Jump," she says and he does, fully clothed.

She is still sitting there and he swims towards her, wishing that the moon would come out and throw light on her face. When he is within handshaking distance, he makes a grab for her bare leg. She is just beyond his reach. He swims closer and she eggs him on, "*Paas, aur paas.* Come to me, my darling. I've been waiting so long for you." As he draws closer, his senses begin to swim in the scent of her perfume. The fragrance is familiar but Suresh can't recall from where. She swims into his arms and he tries to kiss her. The alcohol on his breath makes her turn her head away. "Since when have you been drinking?" He knows that voice. But before he can react, her hands reach out to hold his head, gently pushing it into the water. After a while, it gets difficult to breathe. Water is flooding into his eyes, nose and mouth. Suresh struggles to break free, but she holds him down in a deadly stranglehold. Just when he thinks he will suffocate, her grip slackens. He comes up for air, gasping. She smiles at him. The moon is out and he can see her face.

"Shahnaz?" he exclaims.

She nods. "You took my horses, my husband and my child. Your wife and you..." Her black eyes glitter with rage.

"No, no! Listen..." She pushes his head down again.

The moon disappears. In the dark, the man in the pool is gurgling, gasping and gulping the chlorine-infused water, trying desperately to escape the young woman's grasp. This time, she holds him down until he stops struggling.

When the moon comes out again, the pool is empty except for Suresh's dead body floating in the water.

A few minutes later, Zoya emerges from the pool, picks up her drink and heads indoors.

***

The next morning, in the villa, Kiara wakes up early and checks on the twins. The girls are sleeping peacefully. Relieved, she shuts the door softly and moves to the next room. Sid is also asleep, but he is moving around restlessly and his face is flushed red. Concerned, she walks up and puts her hand on his forehead. He is running a temperature and cries out in his sleep. "Mamma, take me away."

She runs to the master bedroom. Aditya is just waking up and tries to pull her into bed. Kiara pushes him away, saying, "I need to talk to you. Now."

Realising that she is upset, he gets out of bed, responding, "Sure, I am listening."

She shakes her head. "Not here. Even walls have ears. Let's take a walk outside."

Aditya is surprised but doesn't argue. Quietly, he follows her out. Kiara hasn't waited to change and is still wearing her attire for the night—a pair of shorts and a tee. She shivers in the early-morning chill. Aditya, who is more warmly dressed in tracks and a jacket he grabbed on the way out, pulls her close, rubbing her bare arms. "What is it? What's wrong, babe?"

Kiara takes her time to answer. "I don't know how to put it, Aditya. But something's not right here. Yes, the property is gorgeous and serene, but there's something simmering beneath—it's the calm before a storm."

Aditya opens his mouth to contradict her, but she gestures for him to keep quiet. "I'm scared, Aditya," she says as she looks over her shoulder at the lodge and shivers. "That house scares me. I've been seeing things—weird things."

Aditya tries to comprehend what she is saying and repeats after her, "Weird? Like how?"

As a montage of all the eerie things that have happened flashes through her mind's eye, Kiara trembles. "I feel a presence in our villa too. The presence of another woman and another child. The woman from the lodge… And just now, Sid was talking about…"

Aditya forces a laugh. "Are you okay, baby?"

Irritated, Kiara pulls away from him. "I need to get away from here. We need to get Sid away. His life is in danger, I can sense it."

"Is it Parzaan?" Aditya asks tentatively. His wife has never behaved so irrationally before, he thinks.

She shakes her head, saying, "I wonder about Parzaan. I wish we could see him, but Sid is not in any danger from him. No, it's someone else," she breaks off abruptly and whimpers, "Let's go back home, Aditya. This doesn't feel like my home anymore. I am an intruder here. Let's go back to our apartment in Mumbai."

Suresh and Suman's warning echoing in his ears, Aditya nods and pulls her back in his arms. "Okay, I will hand the property over to Sunny and his team. Once they start their work, we will leave. I promise, it won't be long. Just a few more days."

Kiara looks relieved and thanks him, apologising for being such a spoilsport. He hugs her, assuring, "No sorry needed, babe. I've told you that often enough." She nods and he continues, "Old houses give out vibes and not always good ones. Not to worry. Once it is remodelled, I will sell the lodge."

She looks concerned. "Will you run into losses?"

He slants her an amused look and tells her she married a whiz kid. "I will make a huge profit from it. More so now that Sid has found us the warehouse," he promises.

His reference to Sid makes Kiara anxious again as she remembers her feverish son calling out to her. "Aditya, Sid..." She is interrupted by Sana calling out from the balcony and telling them that Sid is awake and crying for his mamma. "I'll be right there," Kiara shouts and quickly walks back towards the house.

Aditya turns to follow but suddenly Madhu turns up. The helper looks agitated. Aditya waits for him to draw closer before asking if anything is amiss. Madhu nods. "*Woh mar gaya.*"

Shocked, Aditya asks him who is dead. Madhu replies, "Suresh. This morning, they found his body floating in the pool."

***

The police have cordoned off the area around the swimming pool at Horseland Hotel. The media is milling around, trying to find out what happened. Suresh's body has been fished out of the water, bagged and put in the ambulance. Suman is standing beside it, wailing loudly and repeatedly saying, "I warned him. He wouldn't listen."

Many of Suresh's friends, mainly ghodawallahs, are silently gathered around her, suddenly afraid for their lives. Tembe shares their apprehension and turns to the inspector, saying, "Sahib, there's a mini train leaving at 12 noon. Let's take it and go back. This place is haunted. *Roz ek wicket gir raha hai.*"

Todkar is watching Aditya make his way towards Suman. She points to Suresh's body covered with a white sheet. He looks shocked and speaks to her softly. The inspector walks up to them.

"Hello. You must be Aditya Malhotra, the new owner of Cecil Lodge. I'm Inspector Todkar. Suman tells me that last evening Suresh went to the lodge to drop you?" Aditya nods and Todkar adds, "Do you have any idea why he would come here on the way home and jump into the pool fully clothed in the cold?"

It is Suman who answers, "It was her. She drew him in. And killed him."

Aditya looks as shocked as the inspector and asks, "You mean Suresh bhai was having an affair?"

Suman doesn't react and just bursts into tears again.

***

At Matheran Hospital, Priya is vomiting—she is very unwell. The doctor advises complete rest. From what he has heard, he suspects the youngsters are doing drugs. Suddenly, Amar bursts into the room, panting heavily. "One more ghodawallah is dead. They found his body floating in the pool of our hotel. I heard it on the news just now when I went to the canteen for a cup of coffee. We didn't know because we came here with Priya early." He turns to Jimmy and beseeches, "We have to leave this place. *Abhi*. Or we will be dead too."

Surprisingly, he nods, saying that they will do so as soon as the doctor gives Priya permission to travel.

17

Puppet on a String

In the dining room of Cecil Lodge, there is a half-melted candle in front of Shahnaz and Parzaan's portrait. After a few seconds, it lights on its own.

Outside, the handle of the foosball bar cranks up the board and the miniature players start kicking the ball.

On the grounds, the merry-go-round begins to rotate slowly, round and round.

Google runs out towards the back, sniffing at the drain. The water is dark, tinged with red.

***

In the bungalow, Kiara gives Sid some pills and watches as he gulps them down. She then tucks him up and tells him that she will read him a story. He pats the bed and she gets in with him, holding him close.

"Sing to me," the little boy mumbles and she starts humming. It's the same song that Suresh had heard the night before.

Her eyes are cloudy and black as she looks down at him.

***

Minutes later, the twins come running into the room. Sara hands her phone to her aunt, saying, "Maasi, see this WhatsApp forward I just received. It's like a negative picture and so cool. You gotta stare fixedly at these three dots for 30 seconds and then look up at the ceiling and you will see the one person on your mind."

Kiara laughs and asks, "And who did you see?"

Sana smiles as she replies, "Mummy."

Kiara looks at her twin inquiringly. Sara blushes deeply and keeps mum. Sana nudges her, giggling, and reveals, "Her boyfriend, Manav, from school. He's sweet on her and she..."

Sara cuts her short, urging Kiara to stare at the dots on the phone. Their intrigued aunt looks down, her eyes hazel again, while the girls count off the seconds. "1 2...10...15...20...30." They point to the ceiling and she looks up. Shahnaz is sitting up there with baby Parzaan on her lap, just like the portrait in the dining room.

Kiara freaks out and looks down at Sid. She sees Parzaan smiling back at her. The girls are giggling and Sara asks, "Isn't it cool?" She springs out of bed, running to the bathroom to splash water on her flushed face. She looks at the mirror and sees the tub behind her slowly filling with water. The door shuts. The lock turns.

The twins are banging on the door, asking her if she is ill. Kiara is deaf to their cries. Slowly, she starts undressing as a bottle of crystal cubes tips into the water, turning the tub foamy and inviting. She climbs into it and lies there, looking up at the ceiling.

The water slowly turns red, as though tinged with Shahnaz's blood.

Kiara sees a montage of images on the ceiling.

Shahnaz rides up to Garbett Point with a handsome young man and makes love with him under a canopy of trees on a sheet of autumn leaves.

Shahnaz gets married on the grounds of Cecil Lodge. It's a winter wedding and she looks lovely in a white off-shoulder dress that looks rather familiar. Her veil, a flimsy strip of red chiffon, can't hide her happiness as the same young man beams down at her. There are only a couple of locals, including Madhu, present at the occasion. From a distance, an old man from one of the portraits watches them, with his face set and his fingers gripping his umbrella.

A fretting Shahnaz, pregnant and huge, paces the room as an elderly woman, obviously a maid, hovers around her.

Shahnaz holds a wailing infant with the care and gentleness of a new mother.

Shahnaz, dull and depressed, sits morosely in her room all alone. Shahnaz, chuckling and happy, sits with Parzaan on the rocking chair as the sound of her laughter rings through the room.

Suddenly, the doorknob turns and Aditya walks in. He sees Kiara in the tub as she looks fixedly at the ceiling and stops short. The girls crowd the doorway.

He turns and looks at them, saying, "Don't worry. Your aunt is fine. I will get her up and dressed. You go to your room."

Sara opens her mouth to argue, but Sana pulls her away. Aditya turns to Kiara; she is looking at him now, her eyes black with anger. "Why did you leave me?"

He cuts her short, saying, "I have some bad news. Suresh bhai is dead. They found his body floating in the pool of a hotel near Garbett. You need to get dressed. The cops will be here soon. I was the last one to see him alive when he came to drop me here last evening. They may want to talk to you too." Quietly, he walks out.

Shahnaz is sitting on the ceiling of the bedroom, smiling. She is humming the same tune that lured Suresh to the pool. Aditya doesn't hear her as he leaves.

***

In the living room, the two cops are seated on straight-backed chairs and Aditya and Kiara are together on the sofa before them. He is anxious and apprehensive while she is relaxed and expressionless.

The inspector is looking around appreciatively. "This is a beautiful property you have here," he tells Aditya, who only nods listlessly. Suresh's death has hit him hard. He was fond of the horseman.

Todkar turns to smile at Kiara, saying, "You must be really happy in your new home, madam?"

Kiara frowns at him, replying, "Why do you say new? *Yeh to hamesha se hi mera ghar hai.* And it will always be my home. Yesterday, today, tomorrow—always."

Her slightly belligerent tone has him sitting up straight. Even Aditya starts. There's a minute or two of silence during which Todkar sips his tea, with his gaze on the couple. Aditya fidgets uneasily, while Kiara stays cool but frowning. Then slowly, the wrinkles on her brow iron out and her smile returns.

"So, what's the plan with this property?" Todkar asks curiously. Before Aditya can tell him how he plans to remodel the lodge and sell it, Kiara jumps in, claiming, "We will live here, of course. There is lots of room for Sid to run around, and we may soon give him another child to play with."

Aditya is stumped, wondering where that came from. Kiara had a really bad pregnancy with Sid and was bedridden for almost six months. Their son was born premature and had been a cranky baby, giving them a hard time until he was three months old. After that, it had become easier, but Kiara had always said that she would never have another child. Sid had his cousins for company, she had said, and Aditya had never pushed her to reconsider. He was happy with Sid.

The inspector is pacing the room. "I'm glad you like it here. I had thought you might get spooked, what with three deaths coming in close succession—that businessman from Mumbai, Manish Shah, Abdul, the guide, and now Suresh. Many tourists can't wait to return home."

In his corner, a disgruntled Tembe mumbles, "I want to as well, but no one listens to me." His voice does not carry.

It suddenly strikes Aditya that Kiara is trying to present a happy family picture so that he is not seen as a suspect in the ghodawallah's unnatural death. He turns to smile at his wife for caring so much. She doesn't smile back. He blusters, "These deaths…they were all accidents…tragic accidents… even Suresh bhai's. There's no link between them."

To his shock, his wife contradicts him. "Of course, there is a link. It's right there in front of everyone's eyes, but it's just that they are blind to it. It's a link screaming to be heard, but everyone has turned a deaf ear to it. It's a link that wants to say so much…" Her voice trails off as Sid calls out from upstairs. Kiara is instantly on her feet, apologetically saying, "You will have to excuse me. My son isn't well today. He has a fever; I need to go to him."

Todkar graciously says, "Of course, I understand, madam. I'm a father too. We will leave today and maybe come back another day." He drains his cup before adding, "Thank you for the excellent tea."

Kiara, who is already halfway up the stairs by this point, pauses. As their eyes meet, hers black and glittering, Todkar shivers involuntarily. The inspector waits till she is on the first floor before raising his voice slightly to say, "Take care of your son, madam. *Mausam kharab hai*. There is a nip in the air and people are falling ill. *Phir milenge jaldi* to discuss the links."

Aditya squirms uneasily, realising that Kiara's carelessly spoken words have aroused the cop's suspicions. "You are welcome to drop by anytime, and if you give us sufficient notice, I can get Madhu to rustle up a meal," he says, trying to curry favour. Only Tembe smiles at the prospect of a free meal.

"Malhotra...*matlab* sahab and memsahab are non-veg," he reminds himself and licks his lips in anticipation while imagining tandoori chicken, seekh kebab and mutton rogan josh in his mind. Todkar doesn't comment, but as he passes through the door, he turns and looks Aditya directly in the eye, warning, "Take care of your son. And your wife. She seemed somewhat disturbed."

Aditya forces a laugh. "No, no, Kiara is fine. It's just that she is still adjusting to the surroundings. It's a new place for her and..."

Tembe, looking puzzled, cuts in, "But she just said this has been her home *hamesha se*."

Aditya doesn't reply, foxed by his wife's strange behaviour. After the cops have gone, he sits in the chair by the window, reflecting on all that has happened since they reached Matheran. It starts rocking gently without him moving. He doesn't notice.

Till he is jolted from his reverie by the sound of a flute being played nearby.

***

An elderly man is walking towards the villa. He has a thatch of white hair, but his face is brown and wizened, courtesy the sun, and his clothes scruffy but clean.

The girls come clattering down the stairs, with Sana excitedly asking, "Uncle, who's playing the flute so beautifully? Is Lord Krishna here?"

Aditya laughs. "I think Krishna is busy fighting the Mahabharat in Mumbai. But, yes, we have a visitor. Let's find out who he is."

He opens the door, with the girls behind him. The stranger tells them that he is the local entertainer. "I play the flute. Do magic tricks. I also have a puppet show. I have been coming to Cecil for years except..." He stops abruptly.

Swallowing the sudden lump in his throat, he continues, "The place has been empty for so long. But if the local gossip is true, Cecil has a new owner now. When I heard that there are kids living here again, I decided to pay a visit. My name is Krishna."

Aditya looks at the twins, and all three burst out laughing as a bemused Krishna looks at them, wondering what he said that was so funny.

Smiling delightedly, Sara pulls up a chair and sits down. "We are ready for your show. I'm glad you came. It was getting really boring."

Sana tells them that she will get Sid, and in two minutes, she is back with Kiara carrying the little boy in her arms. The man greets her with a "namaste" and soon has the kids laughing with his card tricks. Watching him deftly shuffle the pack and pull out cards, all seemingly randomly, Aditya admits that he is good.

The man then makes the water in his jug flow out in a steady stream, telling them that this is the water of India. "It never dries up."

He pulls out a coin from Sid's ear and, tapping his stick, gallantly offers Sara the red rose that appears at the end of it. Sana also gets a rose—a white one which grows out of her head.

Aditya soon gets into the spirit, his encounter with the cops and Kiara's faux paus forgotten. His wife, on the other hand, goes into a trance as the puppet show begins.

One of the puppets is Shahnaz and the other is Amit. The former is angry. "Why do you have to go now with the baby on the way?" He promises her that he will be back soon. "This is my home and I have Papa, you and Parzaan. We will soon be together and I will never go away again. Just a few more months, jaan." She shakes her head, saying, "I hope you won't be too late."

Suddenly, Kiara hears a gun go off, jolting her back to her surroundings. The children are clapping. She hears Sara say, "That was fun—Red Riding Hood told through puppets, with the hunter killing the granny wolf at the end."

Sana nods, adding, "And he deserves it too."

Krishna laughs, promising to return. Sana nudges her twin. "Maybe Cinderella or Sleeping Beauty. In both of them, the prince kisses the girl awake. Maybe we can get Manav to..."

Sara hisses, "Shut up, you." Anticipating her next move, Sana runs off, her sister chasing after her.

Laughing, Aditya digs out a few rupee notes and holds them out to Kiara. "Well, I have my Sleeping Beauty right here with me. Wake up, the show is over. Give Krishna the money," he tells her with a teasing laugh. She smiles and hands the money over. The magician's eyes are shimmering with tears.

Aditya is instantly concerned. "Are you okay?"

Krishna nods, saying, "Yes, yes, I am fine. It's just that I have returned to Cecil after a while."

He looks at Sid snuggling in his mother's lap and softly says, "I once performed for a little boy. He was around one. Parzaan baba. He would be your son's age now and the memsahib reminds me of Shahnaz madam."

Kiara smiles and replies, "Thank you, Krishna. We are meeting after six years. After that birthday party."

Aditya and the twins turn to her in surprise. How could she have met Krishna? This is her first trip to Matheran. Perhaps, she had come down from Mumbai for some child's birthday.

Krishna freezes, looking at the mother and child.

***

In the hospital, Amar and Zoya are settling the bill. They had to bring Priya in last night when the fever escalated. The doctors put her on an antibiotics drip and kept her overnight. The two stayed with her. Now, she is ready to be discharged and Jimmy has decided that they will be returning to Mumbai on the next train. In her room, Priya is ready and waiting. She is a bit pale and weak but otherwise okay. The door opens and she looks in its direction. Her eyes open wide and her pupils dilate. One side of her body starts twitching, and she falls back on the bed. She tries to scream, but no words come out. Her hands clutch her throat and Priya writhes in agony. Her eyes are rolling back and her body is turning blue.

Jimmy walks in, takes one look at her and screams for the doctor and nurse. They run in and give Priya an injection. After a few minutes, she calms down and the doctor turns to Jimmy, his face rather grave. "She has suffered a paralytic stroke. I don't know why that happened, but my advice would be to take her to Karjat or Mumbai if she can make the trip. They have better facilities."

Jimmy nods, anxiously asking, "We will get her the best doctor, *par theek toh ho jayegi na*? I love her and I can't live without her."

The doctor looks at the boy sympathetically. "It's difficult to say anything right now, but don't give up hope. Love can work miracles."

Zoya and Amar are still at the reception, blissfully unaware of what has happened until Jimmy staggers out, hollering to them from across the hall. "Priya's had a stroke, a paralytic stroke." He breaks down.

Zoya flies across the room to take him in her arms, murmuring, "There there. You have me…Us."

Amar looks down at the two of them, trying to bank down the flames of jealousy. After a moment, he sits down beside them and takes Jimmy's hand. It is ice cold. Half an hour later, the youngsters leave in an ambulance, its siren screeching. Only one vehicle is allowed in Matheran.

18

Down Memory Lane

At Khan's restaurant the cops are finishing lunch while the old man is playing carrom with his grandson. Finishing the last of his biryani, Todkar walks up to them and says, laughingly, "Khan sahab, how long will you keep defeating a child? *Ek* game *mere saath ho jaaye*? I used to be the champion of carrom in college."

Khan gestures to Shazia to take her son away and invites the inspector to take the chair opposite him. As they start playing, Tembe joins them, solicitously asking, "Is your wife better now, Khan sahab? Don't worry. You are not alone. Other people's wives are also suffering from mental problems these days."

As Khan turns to him sharply, Tembe says, "Aditya sir—Cecil's new owner. *Uski biwi bhi kuch*..." He holds a finger to the side of his head and makes circles indicating that Kiara is crazy.

Khan looks alarmed and inquires, "What happened to his wife?"

Todkar sinks the Queen and jubilantly says, "Khan sahab, *aap toh gela*. This game is mine now." The old man is completely disinterested in the game, but the inspector is interested in learning more about the lodge's history. "That lodge...*Kuch* mystery *hai wahan*. If anyone would know, it's you. Didn't you say your wife worked there once before?"

Khan calls out to Shazia to get them some tea. Tembe whoops in delight, saying, "Lunch *ke baad chai* compulsory, just like after getting the *rani*, it's essential to take cover."

After tea is served and the game forgotten, the other man softly says, "At one time, Cecil was the number one hotel in Matheran. *Sab jalte the* Irani sahab *se*. He was Iron Man, and as long as he was the boss, business flourished. But with age, his mind started fading."

"Alzheimer's?" Todkar interjects and Khan shakes his head, saying, "*Nahin*...Sizo *kuch*."

The inspector nods. "Schizophrenia. It's a kind of mental disease."

There is a long pause that culminates in the old man sighing. He says, "*Haan, par unhe* mental hospital *nahin jaana tha*. Shahnaz beti *ne bahut* convince *karne ki koshish ki*. She wanted to take him to Mumbai for treatment, but the old man wouldn't go. So, finally, she called a doctor home, but he even drove away the psycho doctor, running after him with a stick and a knife."

Tembe sips the tea appreciatively. "*Masala chai wah, mast*!" Todkar gives him an exasperated look.

Khan is lost in his memories. "*Dheere dheere* the lodge started going into losses. Shahnaz beti tried to keep it running, but it was difficult for her. No one wanted to work there because Irani sahab's moods had become so unpredictable. One minute, he would be talking to you nicely, the next minute he would get violently abusive, accusing you of spying on him and stealing his money. The locals started steering clear of Cecil."

Todkar tries to imagine the young girl with her mentally ill father and his heart breaks. "Didn't friends and family pitch in to help?"

The elderly man sitting opposite him laughs cynically. "Friends and family stay with you only as long as everything is going well. But when there's a mentally ill person in the house, they stay away." He glances towards his wife's room sorrowfully and falls silent.

After waiting for a while, Todkar prods gently, "*Phir*?"

Khan puffs on his hookah before saying, "Then Amit sahab came to the lodge. He was on vacation here. They fell in love. He married her, but he was not a Parsi, so the community boycotted the family. Her husband was in the merchant navy. His career took him away. She was all alone—pregnant and with a mentally ill father. He died. She died. *Sab mar gaye* and yet they are still alive."

The constable pales at the thought and looks at Todkar. "Sahib, *char baje ka* mini train *hai*. In my opinion, we should leave today."

Todkar looks at him with irritation and retorts, "Shut up, Tembe." He turns to Khan. "You said your wife worked at the lodge?"

Just at that moment, the azan begins and the old man gets to his feet, saying it is time for his prayers. Leaning heavily on his stick, he limps away somewhat hurriedly. Todkar looks after him and sighs. "I was so close to cracking the mystery. Now, we will have to wait for another opportunity."

Tembe nudges him. "Sahib, should I book tickets online?"

***

It's dusk and Charlotte Lake is shrouded in mist. Madhu hurries into the woods where the aghori baba is sitting in front of the unlit fire. He lights it and the old man starts the havan.

Baba keeps giving stuff to Madhu to throw into the flames. At the end of the ritual, he ties a black thread around Madhu's biceps, saying, "It will protect you."

The helper thanks him, asking, "You are sure this will keep her away?"

Baba says, "You can't be sure of anything in this world. This is the only *kawach*—protective shield—that I can give you."

Madhu sighs. "Well, it's only a couple of more days. Memsahib has convinced Aditya sahab that they should go back to Mumbai. They are waiting to hand the place over to the workmen. Once they leave, I will stay away too and will just bring the workers food twice a day." He turns and slowly walks towards the lodge.

***

Back at the bungalow, Kiara is in Sid's room to pack his clothes into a suitcase. The boy is playing PubG in a sulk as his parents are taking him away from Parzaan.

In the next room, the girls are putting away their things. Sana whines, "Why do we have to leave? I am growing to like it here."

Sara looks at her in surprise. "How can you like it? This place is dead. I can't wait to get back to the city lights and our friends."

Aditya is sitting on the balcony, smoking. Kiara comes and stands behind him, looking up at the moon. "It's so beautiful here, yet..."

He smiles up at her, saying, "Not more beautiful than my *jaan*."

She drops on her husband's lap and puts her head on his shoulder. His hand snakes around her waist before he draws her closer. "Tomorrow, by this time, we will be back in

Mumbai. It's good that Sunny managed to round up his men and materials so quickly. Once I have given him a tour of the place, we will leave. I will come back for some of our things later. You don't need to be back, ever."

Kiara nibbles on his earlobe. "What will you do with this place?"

Aditya nuzzles her neck, explaining, "I will clean it up, make it nice and comfy and put it up in the market again. For now, I think we should retire to the bedroom and lock the door."

Kiara laughs a soft, sexy laugh. "Sid is asleep."

His lips move lower as he flicks open her shirt's buttons. "Yeah, but the girls are still up. I don't want anyone interrupting us."

***

A couple of hours later, the door to room no. 19 in the lodge opens silently. The windchimes tinkle and the clock strikes 12. A gust of wind blows down the dimly lit corridor as a presence makes its way out.

The knob to the main door of the villa turns. The living room is dimly lit. Aditya has passed out on the sofa, with his laptop screen showing architectural diagrams. The house is silent as everyone is asleep.

The presence walks up the stairs and steals into Sid's room. The boy is huddled under the quilt, which promptly pulls away. The window opens a crack, and as the cold touches him, Sid mumbles his annoyance. He pulls the quilt over him. A minute later, his bed starts shaking gently before the movements turn more vigorous.

The little boy wakes up, his eyes wide with shock. In the blue light of the night lamp, he sees the body of a woman hanging from the fan above. It is static for a minute before the blades start to rotate and the body begins circling over him.

The bed is jerking, the wind is howling and the woman's body is moving faster and faster. Sid is shocked into silence, but his bedroom door bangs shut. The noise resonates through the too quiet house.

Aditya wakes up and runs up the stairs. At the top, he sees Sara looking ghostly white out of fear. She points to Sid's room and whispers, "There's someone in there, Masa. I heard noises."

Aditya puts his shoulder against the door. After a few hard shoves, the latch gives way and the door swings open. There's a huge black monkey sitting by the open window. It snarls menacingly. Aditya picks up Sid's cricket bat and runs towards it. The monkey jumps off and thuds away.

Aditya hurries to the bed and hugs Sid. The boy is dazed. He looks up at the fan, which is stationary now. There's no dead body there. He shivers as his father pulls him closer. Was it a dream?

"Don't be scared. It was just a monkey. I think Mamma didn't shut the window properly, due to which the wind blew it open and the *langoor* snuck in. No harm done. You are still in one piece, huh? Now sleep. Papa's with you. There's no one around for miles," Aditya whispers in Sid's ear.

He's wrong. Bingo trots out of the woods. Only Madhu sees him.

***

In the master bedroom, Kiara is fast asleep. A drop of blood falls on her forehead. Her eyes fly open, looking up straight. There is no one there. She puts her hand up to her forehead. The blood leaves a reddish tinge on her skin.

She looks to her right for Aditya, but he's not there. She reaches out and switches on the light. The room is empty.

In a white nightgown, she pads out into the corridor. The door to the twins' bedroom is shut, but the one to Sid's is open. She enters and sees father and son sleeping together. Silently, she walks on and picks up Sid. He wakes up with a start. Kiara puts a finger to her lips, motioning to him to be quiet. She walks out of the bungalow and hurries towards the lodge, the little boy in her arms.

Back in Sid's bedroom, the door creaks. Aditya wakes up to discover that Sid is not in bed. He runs out. The master bedroom's door is open. The bed is empty and Kiara is missing too. He rushes to the twins' room. They are gone too. Terrified, he runs down the stairs to find the main door open.

Aditya sees the twins ahead of him and runs to catch up with them. Hearing his footsteps, Sara turns, terrified. Her breath comes out in a rush. "Oh, Uncle, it's you. Thank God!"

He frowns down at them. "What are you two doing out in the cold without even a jacket in the dead of the night?"

Sana speaks up, shivering uncontrollably. "I had got up to go to the washroom. When going back to bed, I wandered over to the window and looked out. I saw a woman come out of the villa. She was holding a boy in her arms."

Aditya interrupts her, his voice sharp with worry. "Did you see her face? Do you know who it was?"

The young girl shakes her head. "No, it was too dark."

He is disappointed. He had hoped that it was Kiara since neither Sid nor she is in bed. Looking at the pale, scared faces of the girls, he forces a laugh. "I thought all of you had taken off for a slumber party without me."

The twins don't laugh, and Sara suddenly pipes up, "We don't know about Masi, but Sana saw Sid."

Aditya pounces on her, saying, "Where? When?" A sudden thought strikes him. "Was he with Madhu?" he asks.

Sana shakes her head. "No, a woman was carrying him. He wasn't crying. In fact, he looked up for a moment, and I can swear he was smiling."

Aditya experiences a rush of relief. He was smiling? That meant he was safe. He must be with his mamma. Where had the two taken off? He looks at Sana and asks, "Okay, baby. In which direction did the other lady go with Sid?"

The girl points a trembling finger towards the lodge, saying, "That way. We were chasing after them."

Aditya gives both a quick hug, tells them that they are both brave little girls and requests them to go back to the villa and wait in the living room. "Let me look for Sid in the lodge. Hopefully, I will find Kiara there too. Maybe, like you both, she also saw the lady and chased after her."

Sara starts coughing and Aditya turns to Sana. "Take your sister and go into the house. It's chilly out here, and I don't want either of you catching a cold. And no matter what, don't step out. Understand?" He hunkers down and looks at them. They nod mutely.

Just then the dark lodge sparkles as lights go on in every room. For a minute, the trio simply looks at it, too amazed to react. Then, Aditya runs off in its direction, shouting for Sid and Kiara.

19

Room No. 19

Kiara is holding Sid close to her and hurrying down the corridor of the lodge. The lights come on and the doors to the rooms on either side slam shut while the windchimes create a racket. She hears Aditya shout out to her and breaks into a run.

Her hair is like a dark halo around her face, and her eyes are a glittering black. Sid stares up at her, but his mamma doesn't look down at him even once. She comes to a stop outside room no. 19. The door opens on its own, but just as she is about to enter, Aditya bursts in, standing down the corridor. She turns and their eyes lock. "Kiara, thank God, I found you both," exclaims Aditya with relief.

To his surprise, she turns away and walks into the room. "Kiara, stop," he screams, running towards her. She doesn't react, but another voice rings out from down the corridor, yelling, "Shahnaz, stop!" Kiara slows down momentarily to turn and snarl at Madhu, clutching a terrified Sid to her breast. The door to room no. 19 shuts behind her.

Aditya runs up and bangs his shoulder against the door, again and again. It remains shut. Madhu is muttering by his side. It takes Aditya a minute to figure out that he is reciting some mantra. Then, from his pocket, Madhu takes out a handful of ash that the baba has given him and rubs it on the door. It opens and Kiara falls at Aditya's feet, as if someone has pushed her out. He bends and picks her up, drawing her close. She looks up at him, her fearful eyes a soft hazel.

Meanwhile, Madhu grabs a rod and dashes in, still chanting. He spots Sid lying unconscious on the ground and carries him out, urgently saying, "*Chalo,* sahab. *Nikalte hain yahan se.* Hurry before she comes after us."

As they run out of the lodge, Aditya notices the twins. They have followed him and are standing outside, shaking and shaken. He grabs their hands and pulls them along. Madhu ushers them into a horse-drawn carriage he has waiting by the gate and picks up the reins. Aditya momentarily wonders how the helper knew that they would need to flee the house, but the thought quickly perishes, at least for now. They are galloping down the road at full speed. The electric poles sizzle and Madhu mutters, "*Saali, peecha kar rahi hai.* We have to get away from her."

As they pass the junction to Sunrise Point and Garbett and whizz past the railway tracks, he lets out his breath, saying, "Phew, *ab* we are safe. She won't follow us. I just hope we are not too late to save Sid baba."

His words render everyone speechless.

***

Half an hour later, they are at Matheran Hospital. A nurse is giving first aid to Kiara who has hurt her hand and banged her head. Sid is still unconscious, though his blood pressure, heartbeat and pulse rate are normal. "He seems to have experienced some kind of shock or trauma. Since you are from Mumbai, I suggest you take him to a hospital there and get an MRI, a CT scan and some other tests done there. He won't get specialised care here," urges the doctor.

Madhu tells them that he will drop them to Dasturi Naka, but that this time they should take an ambulance. "It will be faster. From there you can take a van to Mumbai. I will call up some friends and book one," he suggests.

Aditya nods gratefully. Something tells him that without Madhu, they would all be dead by now. As they part ways, he tries to give Madhu some money. The man refuses, saying, "It was my duty to save you. You are my employer—my *mai baap*. I just hope Sid baba recovers soon."

Guilt-stricken, Aditya remembers how he had been assuming all this while that Madhu was up to no good. The helper, however, revealed en route how he had gone into the house looking for Aditya and come upon Kiara in the grips of a nightmare. "I heard her call out Shahnaz's name and I knew you all were in danger from the spirit. I've been going to a baba for years. His *pooja* has kept Shahnaz away, though it means slaughtering kid goats and chicken. But *kya karen*? No other option."

Aditya winces at the thought of animal sacrifice but feels too weak to voice his disapproval. Instead, he asks the question that has been bothering him for quite a while. "Where's Shivaji?"

Madhu looks at him sorrowfully, saying, "He died, perhaps of Covid. Or maybe *she* killed him too. I'm still alive, thanks to baba."

***

Cecil Lodge is silent and dark again until a burst of psychotic laughter suddenly comes out of room no. 19. It grows louder and louder before slowly fading away as Shahnaz, in a soft and low voice, says, "Parzaan, go to sleep now. Let me sing to you."

She starts humming. It's the same song that Suresh had heard. Its echo can be heard in the van speeding down the ghats.

The twins cling onto each other, while Aditya puts his arms around Kiara. She is clutching Sid, who is still unconscious.

***

Next morning, Aditya and Kiara are sitting in the waiting room of a Mumbai hospital while various tests are being conducted on Sid. Adhish and Sonal, the twins' parents, are with them.

Suddenly, the gadgets attached to Sid start buzzing, their lights flickering and sending strange notifications. A couple of nurses come running out of his room, soon returning with a team of senior doctors. A distraught Aditya waylays them, exclaiming, "What's wrong? Has anything happened to my son?" They brush past him without responding.

Kiara bursts into tears. Sonal envelopes her in her arms, telling her to believe in God. "Sid will be fine," she reassures.

Inside, the situation is grim. The doctors can see that Sid is sinking fast despite their best attempts to save him. "We are losing him," admits one of the nurses, checking his vitals. The doctors exchange alarmed looks, and after five minutes, the senior-most among them, Dr Anil Pathak, comes out looking grave.

He invites Aditya and Kiara to his consulting room. He waits till they are seated before asking again, "You say you saw Siddharth lying on the floor of the room. Did he fall or did someone hit him on the head?"

Aditya repeats what he has been saying since he brought his son to the hospital. "I have no idea what happened inside the room, doc. Nor does my wife. We woke up to find him missing. His cousins saw a woman hurrying away with him. She disappeared, leaving him on the floor of that room. He has been unconscious since then."

It's an abbreviated version of what really happened in Matheran, but he doesn't think anyone will believe the real account. Besides, if he mentions that Kiara was the one who took him into the room, they might believe that it was she who hurt Sid. He knows that it wasn't his wife; it was Shahnaz. So he edits the information he relays to protect his wife.

"How's my son?" Kiara asks apprehensively.

The doctor shakes his head. "At the moment, all I can tell you is that he has slipped into a coma. I won't try to hide from you that we could be in danger of losing him."

Hearing this, Kiara starts sobbing. "No, we can't lose him. Sid is our only son. He came to us after five years of marriage. We visited hundreds of temples and the clinics of all the city's best gynaecologists. We don't know what worked, but after a long wait, Sid was born. He is our miracle baby. We can't lose him," she reiterates.

Aditya is also shocked but is trying to clamp down on his emotions and understand the situation. "What's wrong with my son?" he asks.

Dr Pathak admits that the doctors are as foxed as they are. "His MRI is normal and so is the CT scan. There is no clot in the brain, no signs of haemorrhage and no blood congestion. We have no clue what caused him to turn comatose. There is nothing more we can do for him except waiting," he sighs, reaching for Aditya's hand.

Kiara's eyes are closed, her hands joined in prayer. "God, please don't take Sid away. I can't live without my baby. Please give him back to me."

The doctor looks at her sympathetically and tells them that the next forty-eight hours are crucial. If he survives them, he could be revived. "Let's not lose hope. Miracles happen and he is a miracle baby," he tells Kiara, taking her hand. It is like a block of ice.

Aditya nods guiltily, wishing that he had listened to his wife and Suresh and left Matheran earlier. They were right—that property is haunted. And now the spirit has Sid, he worries.

***

In Matheran, Madhu is locking up the main gate of Cecil Lodge when a hand-pulled rickshaw drives up with two cops. Todkar jumps off even before the rickshaw has stopped and hurries to Madhu, saying, "*Kyun bhai*? Why are you locking up here? Where is Aditya sahab and his family?"

Madhu's eyes are flitting around wildly like those of a caged animal. He has been steering clear of the cops lately and wishes that he had either not shown up at the lodge or left ten minutes ago. Here he is now, being collared by the policewallahs.

He looks up to find Todkar eyeing him expectantly and says, "*Chale gaye woh*. Left Matheran for good."

Tembe, who has walked up, shrieks, "*Chale gaye? Kab? Kahan? Kyun?*"

Madhu looks down the road, remembering their last frantic *ghoda-gaadi* ride. "Last night."

This time, Todkar reacts faster. "Aditya sahab didn't say anything about leaving Matheran when I was here last. In fact, his missus was talking of settling down at the lodge. Why did they suddenly take off in the middle of the night?"

Looking intensely afraid, Tembe says, "Sahib, maybe they fled from the ghost. Thank God they got away. Otherwise, Aditya sahab might have met with the same fate as those ghodawallahs. Sahib, *hum bhi chalte hain vapas* Mumbai. *Char baje ka* mini train *hai.* It is not safe here."

His boss ignores him, his eyes on Madhu. "What happened last night?"

The helper looks towards the woods and remains silent.

The inspector, not intending to let him off the hook, repeats, "*Main kuch pooch raha hoon ki kal raat kya hua*? If you don't answer me, I am going to throw you into the lock-up."

That threat makes Madhu tremble and, folding his hands, he beseeches, "Sahab, *maine kuch nahin kiya.* You can ask Aditya sahab. Why would you jail me for saving their lives? You should also leave while you still can. Before *she…*"

He breaks off abruptly, casting a terrified glance towards the house, and then repeats, "*Aap nikal jao,* sahab. I am also leaving for Karjat. *Idhar rehna* safe *nahi hai.* We must leave Matheran."

Tembe nods in agreement, saying, "I have also been telling sahib that we should return to Mumbai. *Bahot ho gaya yeh* investigation. *Jaan hai toh jahan hai.*"

Todkar rounds on him angrily, yelling, "*Chup kar, saale.* If you want to leave, get lost. I am staying here till I get to the bottom of these mysterious deaths. And I need to know why Aditya sahab and his family left this goddamn hill station in the middle of the night."

Madhu shakes his head and softly says, "Even if I told you why, you would not believe me, so why waste my breath."

He turns to leave but Todkar grabs his arm and yanks him back, saying, "I have to know, Madhu. Who is behind all these deaths? I know you know. I promise not to laugh or mock you."

For a while, it seems that Madhu won't reply. But he eventually says, "*Dekho,* sahab. We are simple folk—poor as dormice. *Hum apna kaam karte hain aur chain ki zindagi jeena chahte hain.* And the only way to do so is to keep our mouths shut. Whenever anyone spoke too much, they didn't live to see another day. *She* is already angry with me, so I don't want to risk my life and neither should you."

Tembe, turning as white as a sheet, runs back to the rickshaw. He beseeches Todkar, saying, "Sahib, *chalte hain jaan bachaye.*"

Madhu nods. "He is right. These are *her* secrets; let them be. Even if you kill me, I won't say another word. Better that you kill me than she does anyway."

He waits a beat for the inspector to respond before walking away. Todkar doesn't stop him. He waits till Madhu disappears down the road and then gets into the rickshaw, asking, "What time is the mini train?"

His deputy beams, responding, "*Char baje.* And we have enough time to grab lunch."

"Okay, we will take it," agrees Todkar before momentarily turning towards the lodge and saying, "But we will be back. I won't rest till I know."

20

The Calls

One month later, at the Mumbai hospital, Sid is still in a special ward. He is no longer on the ventilator, but he is in a vegetative state. Dr Pathak has become a family friend and is constantly reassuring.

"Don't give up hope. We certainly haven't. This kind of a case is rare but not uncommon. It is known to happen with elderly patients," he repeatedly tells Aditya, who seems to have aged overnight.

The doctor explains that due to some kind of a shock, it is possible that Sid's heart had stopped pumping for a few minutes on that unfortunate night. "And in that time, the blood supply to the brain also ceased. That could be the reason he went into a coma."

Aditya is not interested in any explanation. He only wants to know if any of those who were once comatose like his son have recovered. The doctor doesn't know how to answer him. "My profession does not allow me to use these terms, but if I were you, I would not lose faith in God and the power of prayers. Miracles do happen," he reiterates, walking away with a heavy heart.

Aditya breaks down, remembering all that has happened in the last four weeks. Sana and Sara have gone back to school, but the twins are no longer the chirpy girls that they once were. They are morose, always talking about Sid. They recall the naughty kid he had once been and feel guilty for fighting with him.

Their mother is often at her sister's place, trying to rescue her from a deep depression. Kiara has lost all interest in life and spends her days weeping for her son, who is lost to the world.

Aditya is lost without his wife and son. He makes innumerable zoom calls to doctors in the US, Germany and Singapore, begging for help. They are also unable to figure out what is wrong with Sid and how to get Kiara back to the world of the living.

Madhu drops by the hospital one day, giving Aditya a handful of ashes and some prasad that the aghori baba has given him. Aditya hasn't thrown away the offerings but relies on medicine and science.

His brother-in-law, Adhish, however, takes Kiara and him to an astrologer who assures them that Sid would be fine in two weeks. Kiara marks off the days on the calendar. On the fifteenth day, as her son continues to lie unresponsive on the hospital bed, she tries to kill herself by slitting her wrist. Fortunately, Sonal finds her before it is too late.

Aditya takes his wife to a psychiatrist. She is on medication now, and he is drowning his sorrow in alcohol. He reminisces about all the drives, vacations, picnics, school annual-day functions and birthday parties that they have enjoyed with Sid. Why did he have to buy Cecil and take his family there? Why didn't he listen to Suresh who had warned him the first day itself about the lodge and urged him all along to leave? Why didn't he heed his wife's instincts? Guilt erodes his soul and leaves a huge hole in his heart that is impossible to fill. It leaves him writhing in excruciating pain.

***

A month later, Aditya and Kiara have brought Sid home. Their little boy lies listless in bed. Kiara only leaves him to visit temples, churches and gurudwaras. Aditya has lost all faith in God.

At night, she often wakes up screaming, the nightmares from Matheran still haunting her. Her cries wake up Aditya, and while the sleeping pills she has been prescribed help her slip under, he is awake all night, drinking. The alcohol is taking a toll. The once handsome man is now a mere shadow of his earlier self. His eyes are bloodshot, ringed with fatigue. He can't focus on the business. He is slowly wasting away.

***

It is now the third month since Sid's return to the house. In his office, Aditya is closeted in a meeting with Sunny. The architect is apologetic as he says, "I know it's a sensitive subject, and I have been warned not to bring it up with you, but what about that lodge in Matheran? Is the Cecil project shelved?"

After a long pause, Aditya says, "I haven't really given that property any thought in months. I can't bear to. But I won't keep you hanging. I promise to let you know about it soon."

Sunny nods and leaves. As soon as the door closes behind him, Aditya's cellphone rings. It's Madhu calling. Aditya mutes the call. The man helped them escape, but Aditya doesn't want to be connected with anything or anyone that reminds him of

Matheran. The phone rings—once, twice, thrice. Aditya refuses to take the calls.

***

Back home, her psychiatrist, Dr Makani, has come to meet Kiara, who puts her phone on silent as she sits down for her session. "I'm very happy with the progress you are making, Kiara. Yes, you still have nightmares, but the fear and disturbing visuals which once took complete hold of you are fading away, albeit slowly," lauds Dr Makani.

The phone on the table vibrates. Kiara leans towards it to see who is calling. The name flashes on the screen: Madhu. Like Aditya, she avoids the call. Meanwhile, the doctor is calling her a fighter, telling her that anyone else would have given herself up to alcohol or medicinal drugs. Kiara thinks of Aditya, who has been drinking too much. She is worried for her husband but still too weak to be of any support to him. Sid is still unresponsive to the treatment. "We should be talking of my son now instead of me," she murmurs guiltily.

Dr Makani pats her hand gently. "Don't be so hard on yourself. You were also in that room with Sid, and the experience left you battered and scarred too. If you are sitting here talking to me, it's because of your never-say-die spirit."

The phone continues to ring as they chat. Twelve missed calls.

***

Aditya is on his way home from the office. The phone vibrates—Madhu is still calling. Eight missed calls. Damn, the man is persistent, he thinks. But no way does he want any connection with Matheran.

Kiara appears to be slowly getting better and the doctor has assured him that she is on the mend. And if his wife is to be believed, Sid is also responding with small muscle spasms. Even Dr Pathak seems enthused. No way is Aditya going to do anything that might jeopardise his family again. He is like a zombie without them—they are his reason to live.

***

At the house, the psychiatrist is assuring Kiara that all will be well soon. "I'm sure Sid will return to you—he loves you. If he had to go away, he would have by now. That he is hanging in there is reason enough to believe. You have to stay strong for Sid and Aditya; they are incomplete without you. Let's continue with the same meds and doses for one more month. Then we will reduce the medication."

Kiara finally cracks a smile. "You really think I am getting better?"

The doctor smiles back, saying, "Yes, I do. I told your husband that too. He is delighted. Aditya really loves you. You are a lucky lady."

She nods. "Yes, I am. And I am beginning to think Sid will get well soon."

The phone vibrates again. Madhu is still calling. They end up discussing him and how he had saved them that night.

***

Aditya pulls up in the driveway and immediately notices a police jeep near the building gate. Todkar and Tembe are standing beside it, obviously waiting for him. He parks his car and walks up to them, wondering why they would drop in on him.

The inspector greets him with a handshake, saying, "Aditya sahab, sorry to bother you. I don't know if you remember us."

Aditya smiles courteously and responds, "Of course, I do. Though it has been a while. What brings you here? I hope there is no trouble at the lodge?"

Todkar smiles reassuringly. "We are not here for any official work. We were in the neighbourhood on another case and thought we would stop by and check on your son. We heard he wasn't well."

Aditya's smile is warm and genuine. "Sid is still in a coma, but we are beginning to believe he may come out of it."

"He will get better. *Bhagwan hai na,*" Todkar asserts.

Aditya invites them to the apartment for tea and *pakoras*. Tembe is instantly interested and exclaims, "*Chai aur pakore*! *Zaroor*, sir." Todkar gives him an exasperated look as they follow their host into the elevator.

Aditya ushers them into the living room and they chat amicably. Kiara brings in the tea and snacks and sits beside her husband on the sofa. He pulls her close before turning to Todkar and asking, "So, have you figured what's happening in Matheran?"

Kiara stiffens and he rubs her back soothingly. Todkar informs them that they followed them back to Mumbai within hours of their departure. "*Mahol kuch theek nahi laga*. Too many weird things happening."

Tembe nods, munching on an onion ring, and says, "*Meri toh phat rahi thi,* sahib! *Kyun jhoot boloon*? I was so scared that I peed my pants outside Cecil that last time when we learnt you all had left."

Todkar looks embarrassed.

Aditya sighs. "I don't believe in ghosts, but something happened to Sid there. We have consulted the best of doctors, psychiatrists and astrologers. If only someone could help our little boy."

Tembe immediately offers an answer. "*Utara,* sahib." The couple sitting in front of him starts, never having heard the word before. He repeats, "*Utara karana hoga.*" Aditya frowns as he asks, "Do you mean exorcism?"

Todkar tries to change the subject, telling him that he would have liked to continue with the investigation and question Madhu. "I am sure that guy knows something," he muses.

As if on cue, Aditya's phone vibrates and he irritably says, "Talk of the devil and the devil calls. It's Madhu. He's been calling me all day."

Kiara informs that he has been calling her too. "I was with Dr Makani and didn't take his calls."

"I didn't take them either. I wonder what he wants," Aditya muses.

Tembe says, "Sometimes, to get what we desperately want, we need to go back to where it all began. You have tried science and medicine. Now it is time to go back to Matheran."

Aditya and Kiara look at him with open-mouthed amazement. Todkar is angry. "*Chup kar, saale,*" he snaps and apologises to the couple. "Don't mind him. He's not been himself since we returned from Matheran. When we were there, he couldn't wait to get away. Now, he is advising you to go back. Uff!"

He collars his subordinate, thanks Kiara for the refreshments and leaves, saying, "*Sab theek ho jayega,* sahab. Keep up your faith."

Tembe waits till they are in the car before whooping, "*Wah,* sahib. Up there, you were talking like Baba Ramdev. *Ekdum gentle gentle.* I love this good cop, bad cop routine, though in my case it is usually dumb cop. We know now that the son is still in a coma. Madam is seeing a *pagal ka* doctor."

"Psychiatrist," the inspector corrects him sharply and Tembe apologetically nods, saying, "*Haan wohi.* And Madhu is calling them, but they won't take his calls, though he was the one who drove them to the hospital and locked up the lodge after them. *Kuch to gadbad hai,* sahib."

After a thoughtful pause, Todkar says, "I'm going back to Matheran. I need to question Khan and his wife. Madhu too. And a few of the locals. The case must be closed."

Tembe looks apprehensive and his boss gently adds, "You don't need to come with me. I will go alone."

The aide looks affronted. "Sahib, you will risk your life and go there *aur main yahan* Alphonso *choosunga*? I'm coming along. *Meri toh shaadi bhi nahin hui hai.*"

Todkar grins cheekily. "Then, we will have to find a *bhootni* for you there. An angry, *ashant* spirit like Shahnaz will do the trick!"

***

Up in the apartment, Kiara is telling Aditya that Dr Makani is happy with the progress she is making when her phone rings again. "It's Madhu. He has been calling me non-stop since the afternoon. Fifteen missed calls," she tells her husband.

Aditya grabs the phone, muttering, "I thought he was calling only me, but he's been bothering you too. I'm going to give him a piece of my mind. He answers the call with visible irritation and says, "Hello, Madhu. Why are you calling memsahib?"

Madhu is apologetic. "Sorry, sahab. But I called you many times too. When you didn't answer I thought I would..."

Aditya interrupts sternly, "I don't want you to call her. Ever. Delete *kar do unka* number *abhi.*"

Madhu is undeterred. "*Kuch zaroori baat karna tha.* I wouldn't have called you unless it was important. Baba is dead."

Aditya stutters. "Dead? How? I mean did *she*..."

"Yes, she killed him. She has become very powerful again. I found him in the woods when I went there for our planned havan. I might have died too, but baba saved me with his dying breath. And before he died, he told me that there is only one way to save Sid baba."

"Save Sid? How?" Aditya asks, holding the phone to his ear.

Kiara tugs on his arm, asking, "What is he saying about saving Sid?"

"He believes that he has found a way to revive Sid."

"If he can do anything for Sid, we must support him."

Aditya nods before speaking into the phone again. "What do we need to do, Madhu? We are ready."

"Go and meet Dr Bishnoi. Baba knew her. She lives in Pune," says Madhu, adding that he'll share her number. He rings off with a request to be updated after the visit. Aditya promises that he will do so.

After the call ends, Kiara shakes Aditya's arm. "Where are you going?"

He tells her about Dr Bishnoi and she declares that she will go with him. When he protests, she firmly says, "I am Sid's mother. He is my life. I am going."

Aditya nods unhappily.

21

Dr Bishnoi

Aditya and Kiara are on their way to meet Dr Bishnoi. She lives near Lavale village in Mulshi Taluka on the outskirts of Pune. Aditya slants a glance at his wife, who is looking out of the window as the car speeds along, seemingly indifferent to everything. But he knows how much Kiara is banking on this stranger to wake up Sid.

However, the disappointments of the past few months, along with her own illness, have made Kiara guarded. She is careful not to raise her hopes too high. That's her way of saving herself from more pain.

As they near Karjat, she turns to him, her hazel eyes clouded. "How much further?" As Aditya scans Google Maps, he remembers the stray pup Google from Matheran. He wonders what happened to him but doesn't mention the dog. Any reference to that ill-fated trip is taboo now. But he can't stop memories from fading in and out. He is pretty sure that Kiara too remembers everything but just doesn't speak about that cursed place.

Aditya returns to the here and now to find his wife frowning at him as she wonders why he has blanked out. "We should be there in a couple of hours, max," he informs her, and almost on cue, their chauffeur tuts his annoyance. "*Gela*! Tyre puncture. Ishhhh."

It takes half an hour to change the tyre and get moving again. But no sooner have they resumed their journey when the driver brakes abruptly. Kiara pitches forward with a startled cry, while Aditya, already exasperated by the delay, swears loudly. "What the hell man! Don't you know how to drive?"

The chauffeur apologises, pointing to the road. "Saw a snake—a big one—crossing the road and braked to avoid running over it."

Aditya frowns as he looks outside. "Where? I can't see anything."

The driver tells him that it has gone into the fields and Kiara mutters, "Bad omen." Aditya pretends he hasn't heard her.

***

Barely ten minutes later, he gets a panicked call from Sonal. His sister-in-law had gone to check on their apartment as per Kiara's wishes, and she saw smoke spiralling from beneath the main door upon reaching the building. "Short circuit," she explains now.

"Thank God that the house was empty and that you weren't staying with Sid there as we had originally planned. I've learnt to trust my wife's hunches now!" Aditya says, giving Kiara a weak smile before hanging up. She doesn't react.

"How bad was the fire?" Kiara asks a moment later, clearly concerned.

He reassures her, saying that Sonal got there in time, so there isn't much damage. But, he admits, had the blaze grown, their home would have been gutted for sure. "It's strange. She was to visit in the afternoon, but since she was passing by the house on her way to the twins' school, Sonal decided to stop by and check," says Aditya, "Don't worry. All's been taken care of."

Kiara's voice is so soft that he has to strain to hear her. "I was in two minds earlier. A part of my brain was telling me to leave Sid at home in his room but another voice from deep inside insisted that I shouldn't. Thank God I made the right choice."

"A mother's instincts," Aditya reasons.

***

At Pimpri-Chinchwad, the couple encounter an unexpected traffic jam. The road is closed for repairs and cars have piled up.

It has been five hours since they left Mumbai, but the journey seems endless.

When Aditya voices the thought, Kiara darkly mutters, "It almost seems like something…or someone…is trying to stop us from reaching Dr Bishnoi."

Aditya replies, "Well, we are almost there now, so we will meet her, come what may."

***

Forty-five minutes later, Aditya and Kiara stop outside a modest bungalow with a letterbox, on which Dr Bishnoi's name is neatly painted. There's a lawn in front, trimmed with flower beds. Bougainvillea, dahlia, marigold, poppy, hibiscus, jasmine, *raat ki rani* and many more are growing together haphazardly but in colourful harmony, giving the place an inviting look. Aditya, who had been expecting something dark and eerie—perhaps with stars and blinking neon lights—is relieved. This place is a simple, ordinary home that gives him positive vibes.

He turns to Kiara and notices that she is staring at the cottage, whose doors and windows are painted white and red. He guesses immediately that the combination has reminded her of Cecil Lodge and their villa, pulling her back to Matheran. He gently murmurs, "This is not Cecil, Kiara. And Dr Bishnoi is not Shahnaz. She is going to help us get Sid back."

After a moment, Kiara nods, desperate to believe him. The craving to hold her son in her arms, prance around with him, answer his endless questions and teach him something new every day is almost a physical pain now. She can't bear it anymore. The endless night has to end.

As they step through the gates, they hear dogs barking. Some are chained inside, others are being attended to by the doctor. Again, a memory of Cecil flashes, but these canines are not threatening like the wild hounds. They were an omen too, maybe a spectre, Aditya realises in retrospect.

Dr Bishnoi is watching them from the window of her clinic. She is in her forties, with a plain face, slightly overweight body and a pleasant smile that draws wounded people and animals to her. She notices instantly that Kiara is badly shaken up. Just looking at that beautiful but distressed face breaks her heart.

The younger woman instinctively realises that someone is gazing at her and looks in the doctor's direction. Their eyes meet and despite the distance separating them, Kiara is comforted. Dr Bishnoi's empathy reaches her in waves, pervading her being and soothing her mangled soul.

***

A tiny man with bright eyes and birdlike movement hops across. He introduces himself as Hari, the doctor's manager. Aditya remembers him from their conversation while fixing the appointment. He escorts them inside the house, leading them into a room which is big, spartan and airy—a haven for lost souls.

Kiara and Aditya take two hard-backed chairs, and the man disappears, returning with two glasses on a tray. It is some kind of a minty sherbet, refreshing and chilled. As Kiara sips it, she feels her insides beginning to heal with its rejuvenating touch. She also feels stronger, ready for battle.

"What kind of doctor is Dr Bishnoi?" she asks Aditya, curious about another person for the first time in months.

"Our didi is a vet," Hari promptly replies and Kiara turns to her husband in outrage. She hisses, "You brought me to a veterinary doc? You think I have become a beast?"

He whispers back, "Now, don't make a scene. I swear I had no idea."

Just then Dr Bishnoi walks into the hall with a couple holding the stray that she has just treated. The pup wags its short, stumpy tail when he spots them. Aditya is reminded of Google again.

"*Yeh kal tak theek ho jayega.* If he is not better by tomorrow, bring Bobo back," the doctor is telling the local couple, who are not too well off. She waives her fee and the duo walks away after thanking her gratefully.

Dr Bishnoi turns to them and greets them with a namaste, her gaze searching their faces. She invites them to follow her, telling Hari to close the clinic for now. Kiara goes further into the house reluctantly, enquiring who else lives there.

Pat comes the answer. "No one, apart from Hari and me and my animal friends."

***

Dr Bishnoi leads them up a flight of stairs and out onto a terrace. There's a small table and four chairs near the parapet. She takes one and gestures for the couple to join her. On the table is a small bronze idol, the size of her palm. It's some kind of devi and raising it to her face, Dr Bishnoi touches it with her forehead, shuts her eyes and feels the vibrations.

Hari comes and places a tray on the table. It has half a dozen lemons, a knife and a box of sindoor. He withdraws soon after. The doctor proceeds to cut one lemon in half, sprinkles a pinch of vermilion on it and holds the circular disc up.

As she looks into it, a woman is reflected in her eyes for a fraction of a second. Even though her features are not clear, the power emanating from her is so strong that it scalds Dr Bishnoi. With a cry of shock and pain, she immediately throws the *nimboo* down from the terrace.

A moment later, her eyes lock on Kiara and she calmly asks, "How's your treatment going?" Kiara is taken aback, wondering if Aditya has confided in her about her sessions with the psychiatrist. He is just as surprised since he hasn't.

When neither of them reply, Dr Bishnoi repeats the query, adding with a smile, "I hope you are feeling better. But you must take your pills regularly. You need to stay strong for your son."

Kiara, who skipped her dose this morning amidst their hurried departure, squirms, her colour high. Aditya reprimands her softly. "You forgot again."

Dr Bishnoi points to a small temple located at the back of the house and says, "Go down the stairs, Kiara. Turn right and then take a left. You will see the mandir ahead of you. If you can't find your way, just call out to Hari and he will take you."

A protective Aditya immediately jumps to his feet, saying, "I will take her."

The doctor waves her hand, indicating that he should sit. "You can't go there. Only women can pray before this goddess."

Kiara leaves them, dragging her feet. She has grown to lean heavily on Aditya since their return to Mumbai and is suddenly terrified of going anywhere alone.

Dr Bishnoi cuts another lemon and holds it up. It's the same woman whom she saw earlier. This time she screams back at her, telling her to leave Sid alone. The doctor throws the lemon away.

Below, Kiara is walking down the hall, her pace slowing as she approaches the temple. She seems to be in a trance. Above her, Aditya is telling Dr Bishnoi, "*Hum bahot pareshan hain.* We don't know what to do. I hope you can help us. Sid is our life."

The doctor gives him a reassuring look, but in her mind she is watching Kiara who has come to an abrupt halt as she gets the first glimpse of the idol. Aditya is still speaking. For some reason, he is eager to unburden himself to this lady, knowing instinctively that if anyone can help them, it would be her.

"I don't know why I bought that property. If I hadn't dragged my family to Cecil Lodge, all this would not have happened. I feel so guilty."

Dr Bishnoi interrupts softly. "Don't blame yourself. *Honi ko kaun taal sakta hai?* This had to happen."

She cuts another lemon and sprinkles sindoor on it. The red vermillion slowly turns black and she turns to Aditya, her complexion ashen. "Your father's name is Prithvi Malhotra and your mother's Adityani Malhotra, right?"

He nods. "Yes, but how did you…"

Dr Bishnoi continues, "You are their only son, and you have one son, Siddharth. Your wife's *rashi* is *yani* and your son is going through *mrityu yog*. He is fighting what seems like a losing battle with *rahu*."

Aditya looks at her google-eyed, repeating, "How did you…" He had not even told Hari the details of their distress.

The doctor cuts and holds up another lemon. There is nothing. She urgently says, "Go down now and see if Kiara is facing the temple or facing us. A lot hinges on which direction she is looking. If she is looking at the devi there, bring her up here. If she is standing with her back to the deity, take her to the car and return alone."

Aditya looks at her nervously. Something in her expression tells him that he needs to follow her instructions to a T. He nods and leaves. As soon as he is out of sight, Bishnoi cuts another lemon.

***

Aditya goes down the stairs, across the hall and steps out to see Kiara standing 15 feet from the temple. She is frozen at the spot like a statue, her eyes wide and staring. Her back is to the temple and the deity.

He is terrified. He looks up at Dr Bishnoi, who gestures to him to take his wife away. He nods and goes to Kiara. She is stiff and unresponsive. Pulling her by her arm, he leads her away. Aditya seats her in the car and returns to the terrace.

Dr Bishnoi is standing there, looking disturbed. "What does all this mean?" he demands to know.

She looks in the direction of the mandir and says softly, "Devi is very powerful. Only a pure and good soul can stand in front of her and withstand her vibrations. If someone is infected with a negative aura, the person can never face the temple for longer than five seconds."

Aditya tries to comprehend what she is saying. "You mean…Kiara is possessed by Shahnaz?"

Dr Bishnoi nods. "Yes and that is the reason your son is not recovering. The spirit who is also a mother is keeping her away from Sid. Perhaps she believes the boy is her son."

Aditya looks at her with a frightened expression. "Will Shahnaz take Sid away from us?"

Dr Bishnoi is quiet for a while before saying, "If Kiara were a weaker woman, she would have done so by now. But your wife is strong and her maternal love has made her stronger. She is fighting to hold on to Sid. I need to see him. I need to see Sid immediately."

Aditya doesn't argue. He simply says, "Will you be going back to Mumbai with us or do you want us to get Sid?"

Dr Bishnoi walks away briskly, saying, "We have no time to waste. I will travel with you."

Aditya sighs with relief. With Dr Bishnoi by his side, he knows that there is still hope for his wife and son. He looks down at the hundreds of cut *nimboos* lying below. So many cases, so much evil vanquished. Together, they will fight this one too.

22

Tug of War

They are back in the car. This time Aditya is sitting in front, next to the chauffeur. Dr Bishnoi is at the back with Kiara. They are sitting on opposite ends. His wife is looking out of the window, her eyes cold and unseeing. The doctor's eyes are closed and she is chanting below her breath, her fingers busily counting her prayer beads. She occasionally sips the sherbet Kiara and Aditya had been served by Hari.

This time there are no roadblocks and they reach Mumbai in less than four hours. Even before the car comes to a complete halt, Kiara steps out and runs to the house. Aditya alights from the car more slowly, holding the door open for Dr Bishnoi, and says, "I guess Kiara is in a hurry to see Sid. This was the first time we left him alone since coming back from Matheran. I called Sonal, her sister, before we began the drive back, telling her to bring him home. We had left our son with Sonal and her family, but he should be upstairs now."

The doctor doesn't speak as they get into the elevator. She is still chanting and fingering her beads, causing the lift man to look at her a couple of times. Aditya spears him with a stern look and the man shifts his gaze immediately. He breaths again only after the two of them exit the lift.

The front door to the apartment is wide open. As Aditya ushers the doctor in, the twins come running out. "We weren't expecting you back so quickly, Masa. We thought you would be away at least for a night," Sara says.

Aditya looks towards the bedroom and tentatively asks, "How's Sid?"

This time, Sana speaks up. "He's still sleeping. But there was a brief moment a few hours ago when his eyes fluttered open."

Sara interjects, "We don't know that."

This prompts Sana to angrily shoot back, "Why won't you believe me? I was with him then and I saw it happen myself. Soon after, Masa called and asked Mummy to bring Sid here."

Dr Bishnoi is looking around the apartment. It is beautifully done up, with Kiara's artistic touch evident in the décor. But she can sense something in the air. She spots some dark patches on the walls and frowns. "What's that?"

Aditya tells her there was a short circuit earlier in the day. "Thankfully, Sonal got here on time else..." He stops as she begins to say something softly to avoid the girls listening in.

"So, she came here, hoping to take the boy away. But Kiara's will is too strong."

She breaks off as Sonal enters the room. Aditya introduces them and after an exchange of pleasantries, his sister-in-law tells him that she has to leave. "My mother-in-law is not keeping well," she explains, adding, "The girls can stay."

Dr Bishnoi shakes her head grimly. "No, take them with you. It's not safe here." Sonal looks surprised, but Aditya nods. So without another word, she gathers up the twins and leaves, saying, "Kiara is in the bedroom with Sid. Sana says he stirred a few hours ago, but since then he has been comatose. If you need anything, give me a call. I have spoken to the electrician, he will be here later in the day, I wasn't expecting you back so soon."

Aditya assures her that he will handle everything, and they get into the elevator. He looks back to see that Dr Bishnoi is still standing in the living room, staring fixedly at something. He can't see anything, but she is looking at a dog. The dog is Google. She bends down to pat it as it circles around her legs, sniffing. In his eyes, she sees a dark presence outside a door painted a sunshine yellow. She looks up straight at the door to Sid's bedroom. It is yellow.

Knowing Aditya is behind her, Dr Bishnoi adjusts her sandal strap and straightens up. She tells him, "When Sid is cured, get him a pet puppy."

Aditya smiles. "Yes, Siddie loves dogs. He always wanted one. I will get him a Schitzu."

The doctor shakes her head. "No, not a pedigree one. Instead, adopt a stray. I can see a stray dog who will become Sid's best friend and protector."

Aditya remembers Google and agrees without question, asking tentatively, "You just said when Sid gets well...Does that mean you..." He can't bring himself to complete the sentence.

Dr Bishnoi puts a hand on his shoulder and softly says, "Have faith in God...And your wife. She looks fragile, but she is a strong woman who can give up her life for her son."

He nods. "Yes, that's my Kiara. She loves Sid and I love them both. They are my world."

***

As soon as Dr Bishnoi enters the child's bedroom, she notices the inverted horseshoe by the door and automatically reaches out and straightens it, asking, "Where did you get this?"

"One of the girls found it in Matheran and brought it back for luck. Sana believes..." he breaks off as the doctor jerks back violently. Her eyes are closed and she can see a horse. A big black stallion standing on his hind legs and neighing. His eyes are bloodshot and he is foaming at the mouth. Bingo! She opens her eyes to see Aditya holding her. His quick response prevented her from hitting the floor.

He anxiously says, "Dr Sandhya, what happened? Are you dizzy?"

She shakes her head reassuringly and takes a few steps towards Sid. But something pushes her out of the room. As Aditya watches in horror, she falls out into the corridor, this time losing her balance entirely and falling in a heap on the floor. Both Aditya and Kiara run out to her. The door slams shut and the lock turns.

Aditya runs back and tries to open the door. It is jammed. He jiggles the handle. It stays firmly shut. He gets agitated, trying to break it open. It doesn't budge.

Dr Bishnoi has got to her feet. She stands there watching him calmly. He races to the drawing room, yelling, "The keys to the room—they are in the drawer here!" He hunts through the drawers. The keys are gone.

Kiara stands there silently, watching him. She looks haunted. She feels the doctor's eyes on her, but her face simply expresses the compassion she feels inside. The ice melts and she grabs the doctor's hand, her eyes flooding with tears. "Help me...Help us," she beseeches.

Holding her hand, Dr Bishnoi draws her to the door, saying, "We have to go in there. Sid needs his mamma. Let's put our combined strength behind it."

Together, they shove against the door. It opens. Aditya, who is watching them, can't believe his eyes.

This is beyond his comprehension.

***

Dr Bishnoi, with Kiara beside her, walks up to the bed and looks down at the boy. A ragtag Joker is lying by his side. She picks it up, closes her eyes and can see Parzaan holding the toy as he is being carried out of the house by someone. She comes out of the trance and opens her eyes. Right behind Kiara, she can feel a dark presence trying to suck out the young mother's life force. Before she can warn her, Kiara sits down on Sid's bed. The figure vanishes.

Dr Bishnoi puts her hand on Sid's forehead. It is burning. She looks down at Kiara and says, "Tell me what happened when you reached Matheran."

***

As Kiara starts speaking about Dasturi Naka and the media gathered there, the trek to Matheran, the horsemen's refusal to take the kids to Cecil Lodge, Suresh coming to their rescue, Shahnaz taking away Sid to the lodge, the dash to safety, Dr Bishnoi sees the whole journey play out in the eyeballs of different animals: the dog Google, the horses Bingo, Badal and Baiju, the snake on the road and the dogs in her clinic.

Kiara ends the narration, saying, "That night, all five of us fled Matheran and returned home. But *tabse* Sid has been like this—he doesn't smile, speak or run around like he used to. He doesn't even move. He just lies there, day after day…" She breaks down. Aditya rushes forward to gather her in his arms. She sobs into his shirt front, wetting it with her tears.

For a long moment, the doctor doesn't speak. When she does, her words turn Aditya's blood cold and have Kiara looking up at her in shock. "You just said that all five of you returned to Mumbai. You are wrong. *Uss raat, paanch nahin, char wapas aaye.* Sid is still there—in room no. 19 of Cecil Lodge. That's why he has been so unresponsive to treatment. The body is just the shell of his being that you see on the bed here."

Slowly meeting the doctor's eyes, Aditya asks, "Does that mean...Is he...Is he lost to us forever then?"

Hearing his words, fresh tears well up in Kiara's eyes and stream down unchecked. She bends over and covers Sid's face with kisses, helplessly insisting, "No, he will wake up. I'm telling you, Siddie will be fine. I am his mother. He can't leave me for another. I won't let him."

Dr Bishnoi takes her time answering. "If what that young girl—was it Sana or perhaps Sara—said back there about Sid opening his eyes is true, it means that Kiara's love is so strong that despite Shahnaz's constant vigil, his soul keeps coming back here. He wants to be home with you."

Kiara looks up at the doctor, her eyes fierce and her chin jutting out obdurately. "I will do everything I can to hold on to my boy. He is mine. No one else's. Tell me what we should do."

Dr Bishnoi says, "We have to go to Matheran. Cecil Lodge, in fact. That's the only way. And I warn you, it's not going to be easy. You could be inviting death."

Kiara doesn't need to think. "I am ready. Without Sid, my life has no meaning."

Aditya nods and says, "So am I. We can't be a family without our son. We belong together and no one is going to take Sid away from us. We won't let them."

23

Back in Cecil

With a comatose Sid in their arms, Aditya, Kiara and Dr Bishnoi get down from the car at Dasturi Naka. It's late in the afternoon. Even though they started out early, there were many roadblocks on the way again on account of traffic jams, a near-fatal crash, a *morcha* and a collapsed bridge. Shahnaz left no stone unturned to stop them from coming into her turf.

Madhu is waiting for them with an ambulance. Aditya and Kiara get in, with the latter protectively holding Sid to her bosom. Madhu helps Dr Bishnoi in. As the driver turns back, saying, "*Salaam*, sahab," Aditya starts. It's Khan. Aditya has often eaten at his restaurant and knows him well.

"Why have you come for us in this weather? Surely, Madhu could have got someone else," he says with worry.

The old man sighs. "My wife insisted. For years, I kept her locked away, spreading the word that she is mentally ill. But it is time to let certain secrets out into the open."

He refuses to say anything more, pressing down on the accelerator and telling Aditya that he won't go inside the lodge but will wait outside in the ambulance with Sid. "Someone has to watch over the child. Even if Madhu tempted a local with the promise of a large sum of money to make this trip, he wouldn't wait once the mayhem started. And it will," he prophesies, his voice full of foreboding.

Once again, there are hurdles. A landslide has blocked the main road, and they have to take a longer route. Then they have to negotiate an uprooted tree, an overflowing river and a sudden storm. There's thunder and lightning, followed by torrential rain, when they finally reach Matheran. Khan can barely see the road ahead, and it slows them down further.

Through it all, Kaira remains still as a statue, as though she is in a trance. Aditya is preparing for the forthcoming fight, mentally, and Madhu, physically. Dr Bishnoi is chanting and Khan is grim.

The raging storm has brought the electricity poles down, and it is now pitch dark. Mall Road is deserted. The shops have closed early and the ghodawallahs and their horses are warm and dry in their homes and stables as the unseasonal rains have kept the tourists indoors. As the ambulance crosses the railway tracks, Kiara jerks up, suddenly alert. Her eyes are wide and there's a fire blazing in them now. She suddenly thrusts the child into Aditya's arms, opens the vehicle's door and jumps off, disappearing into the dark.

"What the hell!" Aditya exclaims, but encumbered by the sleeping Sid, he can't give chase. Yelling at Khan to stop, he turns to Madhu and instructs, "Go after her."

Before the helper can get out, Dr Bishnoi clamps his hand, saying, "No, let her go. Kiara's love for Sid and her desperation to get her child back have made her strong. Let them face each other. We need to get to the lodge and try to get to the secret. We are losing Sid with every passing minute."

Reluctantly, Aditya tells Khan to keep driving.

***

Room no. 19 is ablaze with light. The commode in the washroom is choked with blood. It flushes automatically and the water rushes down the drain and out, forming a protective circle around the lodge as if to keep visitors at bay.

Creepers twine around the main door and the back exit, locking them off. Big black monkeys are screeching and leaping around the campus. In the forest, a horse is neighing and a pack of wild hounds are howling. The merry-go-round whizzes, and the swings dance in the wind. A huge tree has fallen across the main gate, obstructing entry into the campus.

"What do we do now?" Khan asks as he slows down in front of the gate. A bat suddenly crashes into the windscreen of the ambulance, shattering it. Khan turns the steering wheel, desperately trying to control the vehicle. For a minute, it seems like the ambulance will turn turtle, taking the passengers down with itself. But with superhuman effort, Khan brings the vehicle to a stop in front of the flickering signboard.

Aditya looks at him gratefully, exclaiming, "Thank you! We owe our lives to you."

The driver responds darkly, "Be prepared for bigger battles."

It's pouring cats and dogs. Madhu hands the doctor an umbrella and holds one over Aditya. They get down, leaving Sid in the front seat with Khan.

Looking at Dr Bishnoi, Aditya tentatively asks, "What do you think?"

She turns towards him before responding, "I think the power is at its destructive peak and will do everything she can to keep us from entering the lodge and getting to the child inside. But my devi is with me." She opens her hand, showing the idol in her palm.

Aditya notices something white fluttering on the roof of Cecil. He points it out to the doctor, who is negotiating her way over the fallen tree. The next moment, hounds come towards her baring their teeth. She looks them straight in the eye and they melt away.

There is a clap of thunder, followed by a blaze of lightning. In the light, they see a woman on the roof in a white dress that clings to her like a second skin. Her hair is blowing around her face, concealing its features. But Aditya can never forget that dress. Kiara had taken him in it that day in the villa, wild and wanton. The memory hasn't faded. "Kiara," he murmurs, suddenly remembering that erotic moment. It's been days since they made love.

Dr Bishnoi looks into the eyes of a large black monkey that is glaring at her. In his eyes, she sees the identity of the woman on the terrace. "No, that's Shahnaz. We have to get to her to get Kiara and Sid back," she says urgently.

Even as Dr Bishnoi is speaking, Shahnaz turns and goes into the lodge.

***

In room no. 19, Shahnaz is sitting by a cradle, humming. It's the same tune Suresh heard on the night of his death. It's the same tune Aditya, Kiara and the twins heard when returning to Mumbai with Sid. Footsteps can be heard noisily approaching the room. She puts a finger to her lips. "Shhh. Parzaan is sleeping."

Shahnaz goes to the door and unlatches it. She sees Aditya down the corridor and slams the door shut. She runs back to the cradle and looks down. Then, with a cry of distress, she flies out of the open window.

***

In the campus, Dr Bishnoi touches the merry-go-round. She can see Shahnaz whizzing past with her infant son, waving to her gaily.

She goes to the swing and touches it. She sees Shahnaz again, singing her baby to sleep.

She walks inside and sees the foosball table. She cranks the handle and the miniature players come to life. She looks around for Parzaan. He is nowhere around, but Sid is watching the game.

She walks into the dining room. She looks up at the portraits. They are all alive. She walks over to the photo of Irani senior and asks, "Where's Parzaan?"

He laughs psychotically, saying, "She took him away."

Aditya dashes into the dining room screaming, his eyes wide and terrified. "Her child is dead. I saw Parzaan's skeleton in the cradle just now in room no. 19. There's no sign of Shahnaz."

Just then Google runs up to them, yapping as he sniffs Aditya's familiar scent. He looks down at the puppy, saying, "Where did you come from?" He tells Dr Bishnoi that the stray had been adopted by Sid and his cousins when they were there.

She bends down and looks into Google's eyes. She can see Shahnaz with Sid. She gets up and tells Aditya, "She's gone for Sid. We have to get him away from her."

***

In the ambulance, Sid stirs. Khan turns towards him, gently stroking his head. "*So jaa,* beta. Wake up only when your parents return for you," he whispers softly.

From the seat behind, a pair of slender arms encircle his neck and a voice whispers in his ear, "He's not going anywhere. He is mine and he stays here—mind, soul and now body too."

Khan starts praying fervently.

Long, talon-like nails pierce through the tender skin of his neck and draw blood as a piece of cloth is wrapped around his neck.

***

Together, Dr Bishnoi and Aditya run towards the ambulance. It is still parked in the same spot. Aditya yanks the door open and Khan falls out. He is dead. He has been strangled with a flimsy red chiffon scarf, which Madhu forgot to bury earlier.

Aditya recoils in horror before peeping into the dark interiors and calling for Sid. The ambulance is empty. Sid has disappeared.

***

Someone bangs on Khan's door. His daughter, Shazia, opens it a crack, peering through the darkness and the rain at two shadowy figures. "*Kaun hain aap*?"

"We are policewallahs. We want to have a word with your mother," Todkar replies.

She shrinks back in fright. "No, no, sahab. You are mistaken. My mother hasn't done anything wrong. She didn't kill anyone."

The inspector's voice is gentle. "You got me wrong. We haven't come to arrest her. We just want to speak to her."

Shazia continues to shake her head. *"Uski dimagi halat theek nahin hai.* Abba doesn't let her speak to anyone."

Before Todkar can answer, Tembe says, "Khan sahab is dead. We heard it on the wireless on our way here."

The girl shrieks. "*Nahin*! That's not true. Abba is with Madhu chacha. He said he needed to help some people and that he would be out late and be back before dawn."

Todkar responds, "I'm afraid it is true. Khan sahab *ab nahin rahe*. But if we have to save those for whom he risked his life on this stormy night, we need to speak to your mother."

Shazia is obdurate. "No, Ammi doesn't speak to anyone."

A voice is heard from behind her. "I will now…I heard them…Khan sahab thought if I kept my mouth shut, we would all be safe—from him and *her*. But now, I'm not going to keep quiet any longer. *Ab koi darr nahin raha*. He is gone and if I don't speak, we will be killed too."

24

Attack & After

Dr Bishnoi is in room no. 19. She can feel Shahnaz here. She moves to the bathroom and looks into the commode, which is filled with blood again. The vibrations are stronger here. She can feel the woman's murderous rage, her desire to kill.

She closes her hand over her deity in her palm and, praying fervently, steps out into the bedroom with her eyes shut. Madhu enters to see a crystal chandelier about to crash on her. He pulls her away in the nick of time and, grabbing her hand, drags her out of the room and the lodge.

As they step outside, Aditya comes running towards them. "I've looked everywhere. There's no sign of Shahnaz or Sid. I wonder where she has gone?" He pants as he bends over trying to catch his breath.

Dr Bishnoi thoughtfully says, "To know that, we need to know what happened in room no. 19 that night which drove Shahnaz round the bend." She turns towards Madhu, who shakes his head in response. "Who would know?"

"There's only one person, but she doesn't speak to anyone. And when she did, Khan sahab used to say *sab bakwas hai... pagal ho gayi hai bechari,*" he rues.

"Who?" Aditya asks urgently.

"Khan's wife, Sumeila."

"Take me to her. I have got to know what happened that night. It's the key to the locked secrets," Dr Bishnoi asserts.

***

In Khan's house, Sumeila sits facing the cops. "Ask me whatever you want. *Aaj mein boloongi.* I won't be afraid of anyone—dead or alive."

Her face streaked with tears, Shazia stands behind and rests her hands protectively on her mother's shoulders. Sumeila looks up and smiles at her daughter reassuringly.

"Khan sahab told us you worked at the lodge?" Todkar begins.

Sumeila nods, explaining, "Yes, after Shahnaz beti had her baba, they called me to help. By then, all her family and friends had moved away."

The inspector remembers Khan telling him how the Iranis had been excommunicated after Shahnaz married Amit. He had also mentioned that with her father suffering from schizophrenia and business being down, the lodge had emptied out. He feels a sudden twinge of pity for the young girl—all alone in the valley with a newborn baby, a mentally ill father and a husband away at sea.

"It was difficult for her," Sumeila nods, reading his thoughts and asking Shazia to go to her son who is sleeping upstairs. The girl shakes her head. "I'm not going anywhere. I'm staying right here with you till Abba re..." she breaks off abruptly, remembering that her father is not coming home ever again.

"Okay. Then get us some tea. I'm not going anywhere either and I could do with a *garam* cup of chai," her mother insists. Shazia leaves reluctantly.

After her daughter exits the room, Sumeila whispers, "I didn't want Shazia to hear, but did Khan sahab also tell you how Shahnaz beti wanted to hurt Parzaan?"

Tembe is shocked. "Hurt her own child? Why? *Baap ke jaise woh bhi pagal ho gayi thi kya*?"

The old lady spears him with a look and reprimands him sternly. "You should not talk that way. No one consciously sets out to turn mad. I never imagined that one day people would call me *"pagal"* too and keep me locked up. I am not insane but Khan sahab didn't want anyone to question me about that night."

The constable apologises profusely, and Sumeila, slightly mollified, tells them that Shahnaz was a sweet but introverted child. Although she grew into a pretty and intelligent girl in her teenage years, she didn't, or couldn't, socialise much. With just a couple of close school friends, whose families moved away over the years, she had grown up rather lonely. Her extended family made up most of her circle, but her cousins, dear confidantes as children, were now all grown up and had their own lives. At twenty-one years old, Shahnaz was preparing to go to the US for an MBA when she met Amit Joshi, six years her senior, who had come to Matheran on a vacation with friends and was staying at the lodge. He was well-travelled, worldly and gregarious—a breath of fresh air that enlivened something in her.

***

On the way to Khan's house, with the dead body beside him, Madhu tells Aditya and Dr Bishnoi that although Amit had taken note of Shahnaz's beauty fairly quickly, it was a chance conversation with her that rendered him utterly enchanted. To everyone's surprise, there were passionate thoughts and firm beliefs underneath her quiet demeanour. Cupid struck and soon ignited a full-blown romance between the two.

A few weeks after Amit left for Mumbai, promising to come back to her soon, Shahnaz discovered that she was pregnant. "He had already gone off to sea by then, but after four months, he came back and married her without telling his family or friends besides his old father," he recounts.

It was a beautiful wedding on the grounds of Cecil. Shahnaz looked ethereal in a white off-shoulder dress. She was madly, hopelessly and desperately in love with him. She couldn't wait to become his wife. And he couldn't wait to make her his.

Shivaji and he brought her father down from his room to the grounds for the ceremony. "Irani sahab rambled on about how Amit and Shahnaz wanted to kill him and grab his property. The younger lot ignored it, given his condition," recalls Madhu.

"Who else was present at the wedding?" Aditya asks and the helper admits that they were the only ones because by then her extended family, who had discovered her pregnancy and her intention to marry the child's non-Parsi father, had cut off all ties with the Iranis.

"Amit sahab and Shahnaz didn't want to leave Irani sahab. So they honeymooned at the lodge and moved into the villa on the campus, with dreams of bringing up their baby there," tells Madhu, recalling how Amit had bought Shahnaz a rocking chair that she placed by the window in the living room of the villa. She would sit there for hours as the time of delivery neared.

Aditya gets goosebumps just thinking of the many times he and Kiara sat on that chair.

Madhu's narration continues. Both Amit and Shahnaz were excited about the child. Over the next four months, he ordered loads of toys and baby clothes online. "We tried to tell him it was inauspicious to do so before the baby arrived. Amused, he ignored the warnings, calling them blind superstitions," Madhu glowers.

The always beaming father-to-be had a merry-go-round installed in the grounds. The seesaw and swings, along with the badminton court, were already there. There was also a carrom board and a table tennis table in the smoker's lounge outside the dining room. He ordered the foosball table because he wanted to use the miniature players to teach his son how to play ball. "He was sure they were going to have a son and let Shahnaz pick the name. She chose Parzaan. Her mother had wanted to name her son that. She had got a daughter instead and had died in childbirth," he says.

"What if I die too?' Shahnaz would ask him anxiously and Amit would reassure her that nothing was going to happen to her or the baby. "You are mine—both of you—and no one can take you away from me," he would say, fiercely and protectively.

Then, Amit had to leave. It was too good a career opportunity to miss. He promised a teary Shahnaz that this would be his last trip. After six months, he would leave the merchant navy, work to revive Cecil to its former glory and settle down in Matheran. Shahnaz begged him not to go, but he reasoned that they needed the money for the baby and the renovation of the lodge to get it up and running again.

"So she had the baby all by herself?" Aditya asks, his heart breaking for the young and lonely Shahnaz.

Madhu nods, remembering how they had got Khan's wife to the lodge to deliver the baby. The labour was long—almost twenty hours—before Parzaan entered the world with a lusty wail.

They had decorated the rooms with pink balloons and ribbons. "When she saw them, she laughed, saying we should have listened to her husband. She was very happy and we managed to give Amit sahab the good news. He promised to be home soon," Madhu narrates.

But from there, everything went downhill. Amit's contract with the shipping company was unexpectedly extended with the outbreak of Covid, which led many countries to shut down their ports. While he was trapped at sea miles away, frustrated with the isolation and depleting supplies, Irani sahab's condition deteriorated severely. The physical and psychological toll of caring for a newborn, comforting her struggling husband, witnessing her father's mental decline and managing the finances of the lodge amid nationwide lockdowns was naturally quite high for a young mother.

***

"Sometime after having the baby, Shahnaz started behaving strangely. Maybe she inherited her father's illness. Or maybe it was just being alone for months in that big, cold lodge, with an ailing father and a child who cried all night and didn't let her sleep. She began to resent them both," Sumeila tells the cops, adding that that was when she was hired.

She remembers how Shahnaz had moved back into her bedroom, room no. 19, with Parzaan. On most mornings, Shahnaz would hand the baby to Sumeila as soon as she reached the lodge, saying, "Throw him in the garbage dump. I can't bear to have him around me anymore. He sent his papa away."

"It would chill my blood to hear her," whispers the old woman. Tembe looks shocked, but Todkar understands that Shahnaz was likely suffering from postpartum depression.

The inspector explains that most new mothers experience "baby blues" such as mood swings and crying spells within the first two-three days of delivery. "They become anxious, irritable, have difficulty sleeping, lose their appetite and feel overwhelmed. The phase can last up to two weeks."

"Hers went on for months," Sumeila informs and the inspector nods, saying that in some cases, the symptoms are more severe and long-lasting and result in postpartum depression or even psychosis. "This can cause disorientation and agitation, graduating to hallucinations, delusions and paranoia and even attempts to harm oneself and the baby," he rattles off from memory, having witnessed his own wife's struggles with some of these symptoms.

While Sumeila doesn't understand the medical jargon, she admits that after giving birth, Shahnaz hardly slept, was always pacing around agitatedly, and would get deeply upset if the baby cried, even briefly.

On one occasion, she tried to strangle her father, insisting that Irani sahab had paid people off to kill Amit, which was why he wasn't returning home. "Didn't Amit speak to her and explain the situation?" Tembe wonders aloud and she explains that he did but that his assurances alleviated her anxiety only temporarily. There was no use reasoning with her after a while.

"What about medicines? Surely her gynaecologist prescribed some?" Todkar questions. Sumeila informs that Shahnaz flushed the pills down the commode. "One day, she threw out the food I had brought, telling me that I was slow-poisoning her," she reminisces, adding that after that incident, Shahnaz wouldn't touch anything until the old woman had tasted it in front of her.

Sumeila admits that she often thought of quitting. But the hotel that Khan and she had invested all their savings into wasn't doing well, and she had no other job opportunity due to the pandemic, which had begun injuring the country's economy by then. But, above all, she felt deeply for Shahnaz, whom she had watched grow up over the years.

With the virus spreading like wildfire, people were shutting themselves up in their homes. Khan refused to let his wife go to the lodge, so she brought Parzaan home with her, afraid Shahnaz might harm him. At the lodge, Shivaji and his cousin Madhu were managing things between them.

"I returned to work after two months, thinking Shahnaz beti would be happy to see her son. But she grabbed him and ran to the terrace. She put him on the parapet, stood right behind him and was about to push him down when Madhu caught her." Her voice chokes at the horror of the act.

After that, Shahnaz was guilt-stricken. She moved back into the villa with Parzaan. This time, Sumeila came to stay with her and was happy to see the way Shahnaz cared for her son, feeding and rocking him to sleep in that chair by the window.

"We even took a photograph of her with the baby and had it put up in the dining room with all the others. She would look at the portraits and smile, saying her family was with her again," the old woman recalls with a bittersweet smile.

But once in a while, Shahnaz experienced relapses.

***

"Once, she picked up her father's hunting rifle and shot a horse dead because it was neighing. After that, Shivaji asked Suresh bhai to take away four of the horses since neither her father nor she rode anymore. Only two remained—Bingo and Sultan—for us to run errands. When she heard this, she screamed that we had stolen them and vowed to take revenge," Madhu tells Aditya and Dr Bishnoi.

On another occasion, she flew into a rage, accusing Madhu of spying on her while she was taking a bath. With a knife in her hand, she might have actually cut his throat had Sumeila not burst in.

On certain nights, she would play with Parzaan on the merry-go-round, the seesaw or the swing. Their laughter would fill the silence and darkness. "The next morning, she would tell Shivaji that she had seen some intruders. On her insistence, he got a pack of hounds to patrol the grounds. There was also a stray that Amit and she had picked up together. Surprisingly, the pup whom your son named Google but whom they called Joy was fearless around the hounds, and they didn't harm it either," says Madhu. Aditya remembers their first day at the lodge when the puppy had drawn the wild pack away and saved their lives. But he wonders that if Google had been around then, shouldn't he have grown by now unless...

Madhu is still speaking. "And then Irani sahab contracted Covid—at least it seemed so, given his symptoms—and died a couple of weeks later. We notified local authorities and they took the body for cremation. Neither was there anyone to perform the last rites according to Parsi customs nor did the government's Covid protocol allow them. Shahnaz's extended family did try to resume contact with her upon hearing the news, but they obviously couldn't visit her due to all the travel restrictions. On Amit's insistence, his father, Sharat Joshi, pulled some strings to travel to Matheran to support his daughter-in-law. Soon after his arrival, however, he discovered that Shahnaz had completely fallen apart. And one night..."

Silent all this while, Dr Bishnoi finally asks, "What happened that night in room no. 19, Madhu?"

He shakes his head and reiterates that only Khan's wife would know. "She used to be a friendly lady, but after that night, she has not left her house," he sighs.

"Then we have to go to her now," Dr Bishnoi says in a resolute voice.

25

The Chase

Back in her house, Sumeila is telling Todkar and Tembe that a couple of weeks after Irani sahab had passed away, Shahnaz prepared a feast for herself: dhanshak, pilaf and custard.

"After dinner, she decided to spend the night in her old room in the lodge because she didn't want her papa to be lonely. She was convinced that his soul had returned there. She took the baby with her," recounts the old woman.

Just at that moment, Shazia returns with the tea and settles beside her mother, holding her hand as she knows how difficult the next bit will be for her to narrate.

Sharat Joshi was in the room next door to hers in the lodge, while Shivaji and Madhu were sleeping in the outhouse. Shahnaz had insisted on Sumeila remaining in the villa, in case she wanted to return there during the night. Used to her mood swings by now, the old woman had agreed but was too restless to sleep.

"With me around, Shahnaz beti had got into the habit of never locking the bedroom door because I would go there several times during the night to check on the little baba. In the lodge too, she left the door open for me and he crept in while beti and the baby were asleep." Unable to go on, Sumeila stops.

"Who? Madhu?" Tembe asks and she shakes her head. "Shivaji?" Todkar wonders aloud, and she shakes her head again, unable to bring the name to her lips. For so long, she had kept the secret within the family.

Shazia now makes the long overdue revelation. "Joshi sahab."

Tembe is astounded with disgust. "Her father-in-law? *Sala harami.*"

Sumeila nods with relief that they do not pounce on her. She has feared being arrested for so long. "Upon hearing desperate cries from her room, I stepped inside to discover that he was trying to force himself on Shahnaz beti. When I tried to get him off her, he slapped me across the face and pushed me away. So I grabbed the hunting rifle off the wall and struck him hard on the head. He staggered out of the room, screaming with pain, and I rushed to Shahnaz's side to comfort her. But a couple of minutes later, she picked up the hunting rifle and ran after him. He took Sultan and she took Bingo. In a panic, I called Shivaji for help and told him what happened, what I had done..." The memories now come flooding in like a tsunami.

***

Madhu, Aditya and Dr Bishnoi have reached the junction of Sunrise Point and Garbett Point. The helper points to Garbett, telling them that Joshi senior rode up that hill that night. "Shivaji and I followed him and Shahnaz. We even had to call Suresh for help. Fortunately, we got through and asked him to come with the horses. We met him halfway but were still late.

We were right at this spot when the first shot rang out from the top of Garbett. Shahnaz was hunting Joshi sahab like prey. She was ablaze with fury," he recalls with a dazed look in his eyes as he returns to that dark night.

"She killed him?" Aditya asks, shocked. Madhu shakes his head, explaining that she missed the mark but spooked both the horses. As a result, Sultan came charging down the slope, with Joshi hanging on for dear life. Still in hot pursuit atop Bingo, Shahnaz rode on.

She reeled off a few more shots. One caught Sultan in the leg. He raised his forelegs and reared up. "Joshi sahab was thrown off. He hit his head against a large boulder and died. Right here—where Manish Shah also died recently. My brother never told me what had set Shahnaz off, but he insisted that we needed to dispose of the body for Sumeila chachi's sake," sighs Madhu, looking at the spot. "*Yeh jagah ab manhoos hai*. So is the hill now. There was a landslide soon after and they cordoned off Garbett. Now, no one goes up or near the railway tracks by the tunnel. It spooks the horses, particularly Bingo."

Shivaji, Madhu and Suresh buried Joshi's body deep in the woods. Sumeila was waiting when they returned with Shahnaz in the wee hours of the next day. She handed the baby over to the mother and left. She was traumatised. "Khan sahab never let her return, and she never left the house after that. So, we got Suman to come and help with the baby," he informs.

When Aditya asks if the cops came calling, Madhu tells him that the matter of Joshi's death was completely hushed up. No one outside the lodge knew of Joshi's arrival since Suresh had brought him to the lodge. He kept his mouth shut, taking the injured Sultan to his stable. Joshi's wife was already deceased and he had no other child besides Amit. "We told the young man that his father had died of Covid. He was utterly distraught. If only he knew his character! Anyway, we then secured his permission for taking the body to one of those makeshift mass cremation sites that had sprung up amid the chaos and fear produced by the virus. Sahab, we were lucky, I suppose, that proper records of the corpses couldn't be maintained. None of Amit's friends and relatives could visit, of course. Their condolences over the phone would have done little to comfort him. As for Bingo, Rahim chacha took him away. The old man had trained the stallion's mother too and considered him a son," Madhu states as he concludes his narration.

"Wonder where Bingo has disappeared," Aditya muses. "I keep hearing sounds of a galloping horse. Even now I can hear him."

"He's here now," says Dr Bishnoi, looking down the road. Minutes later, a big black stallion with bloodshot eyes and a foamy mouth appears out of the darkness.

***

Meanwhile, Sumeila tells the cops that she was too terrified to go back to the lodge after learning that Joshi was dead. He had connections and her husband was scared that he may have made some calls to friends, even his son, on the night he died.

"For months, we were afraid of strangers turning up at our door with the intention to hurt or maybe even kill us. We even sent Shazia and her son, who had come here after her husband's death, to my sister's place in Karjat. Khan sahab was also afraid that the police might suspect me of killing Joshi and arrest me. So I stayed under strict house arrest for weeks, which became months, which turned into over two years. The nightmares and the dread that never went away slowly began to affect my mind, and I was prescribed medication to cope with it," she shares.

"I have to know what happened to Shahnaz and her son," Todkar says urgently. "Who would know?"

Sumeila says that Suresh's wife Suman was employed after she left. The inspector immediately jumps to his feet, saying that he has to meet her. Thanking Sumeila, he tells Shazia to lock the door behind them and not open it for anyone. "We will be back with Khan sahab's body later in the night. Till then, stay safe." Both ladies nod apprehensively as the cops charge out and jump onto their horse carriage. Rahim chacha is driving it.

***

Kiara, fully drenched, is walking through the thicket like a dark shadow. She can hear the sounds of snakes hissing, monkeys swinging from the branches and the skies thundering. On any other day, she would have been terrified. But today, her eyes are focused and her brain is alert.

She steps out. The railway tracks are in front of her. There is no one there. She waits in the shadows patiently. And then she sees her…

***

Suman is in the stable. After Suresh's death, her children, who had come to Matheran for the funeral, wanted her to sell the house and the horses and move to Mumbai with them. She had refused. "I have to get to the one who killed your father. My husband was not an ideal man, but I loved him anyway. If I leave now, his memory will remain tarnished forever," she had argued.

When the children later pointed out that he had been found floating in a hotel swimming pool, she insisted that Shahnaz had lured him there. "She set fire to our stable and killed all our horses. We tried to get them out, but she wouldn't let us get close. She had made a circle of blood around the stables," she stated. They left her, thinking that their mother was losing her mind.

But Suman is perfectly sane. She knows Shahnaz was responsible for her husband's death. For all their fights, she still misses him. Perhaps Shahnaz thought that Suresh would tell Aditya sahab to leave the property with his wife and son. So she lured him to the hotel that night, Suman is certain.

"He could swim and the only way he could have drowned was if someone held his head under the water," Suman, who spends most of her waking moments in the stable, tells the horses. She knows now that this was Suresh's refuge from the world. The horses can be very calming and comforting. But today they are skittish, as if they are waiting for something… or someone.

Suddenly, the stable door opens.

***

Bingo sees Dr Bishnoi standing in the middle of the road, a faint white figure in violet light. He charges towards her. She doesn't move.

He is now approaching head-on, with bloodshot eyes and foam dripping from the mouth, as he gains ground swiftly with purposeful strides. Aditya and Madhu try to pull her away, but Dr Bishnoi refuses to budge, warning them all the same to steer clear of the horse. They watch fearfully from the side of the road.

At one point it seems like Bingo will knock Dr Bishnoi down and trample her. But she stays her ground, staring him straight in the eye.

When he is just two feet away, Bingo lifts his forelegs and neighs, coming to a halt at the spot. Dr Bishnoi walks up to him. Stroking him gently, she calms him down. In his eyes, she sees the railway tracks. A woman is walking along them, holding something in her hands. She can hear the sound of an approaching train. She continues unafraid, heading straight for the tunnel.

Bingo neighs, shaking his head. Dr Bishnoi holds him firmly, still reading the past in his eyes, wherein the woman appears to leave the bundle at the mouth of the tunnel and walk away seconds before the train comes out. As it mows down the bundle, a painful cry rings out—a baby's cry.

She strokes Bingo's mane and murmurs to him gently before turning towards Aditya and Madhu. She takes care not to run as that would spook the horse. She gestures towards the waiting ambulance. Once they are seated, with Madhu at the wheel, she urgently says, "Drive to the railway tracks."

Aditya looks at her hopefully. "Is Kiara there? Sid?"

"Yes, they are there. But I hope we are in time to save them because Shahnaz is there too."

Bingo streaks past them. He is headed in the same direction.

26

The Confrontation

Kiara is running towards the woman who is carrying something in her arms and walking towards the tunnel. She instinctively knows that it's Sid. Both the women can hear the sound of the approaching train.

In the darkness and rain, Kiara slips and falls. But she pulls herself up and charges ahead, screaming, "No, Shahnaz! No! Don't leave Sid there. The train will crush him just like it did Parzaan."

At the sound of her son's name, Shahnaz looks in her direction and snarls, holding a motionless Sid close to her bosom. "He's mine. No one gets him even if I have to kill him to keep him with me."

They are within handshaking distance. Kiara's eyes are flat and dull. "You could not keep your own son. How will you keep mine?" she inquires plainly.

Just as the train comes out of the tunnel, she launches herself like a rocket towards Shahnaz. Suddenly taken by surprise, the other woman throws Sid back at her in a reflex response to protect herself. Kiara grabs hold of the child and throws herself to the right of the tracks.

The train bears down, obliterating everything in its way.

***

The two cops are now with Suman in the stable, and she is telling them how after Joshi's death, Shahnaz grew violently aggressive and would lock herself in room no. 19 for hours on end. When she emerged, she'd break things and abuse and threaten anyone and everyone in sight, going on a serious rampage. They learnt to keep out of her way.

"I was taking care of the baby and kept him away from his mother, who hated everyone including him. But one late afternoon, while I was busy in the kitchen and Shivaji and Madhu were in the woods with Parzaan, she mounted Bingo and just took off with the baby," she recounts.

The two men immediately followed her but couldn't keep up. They searched for her everywhere, going all the way up to Garbett. But she had just vanished and was nowhere to be seen. Late that night, Suman was on her way home when she saw Shahnaz crawling on the railway tracks, looking for something. "I called out to her, but she screamed at me to stay away. I ran off to fetch Suresh. By the time we returned, she was holding a bundle in her hands—the badly mangled body of Parzaan baba. She had left him at the mouth of the tunnel and the train had ploughed him down," recalls Suman before breaking down.

Something inside Todkar makes him say, "We need to go there now. Another child's life is in danger. And we need you to come with us."

To his relief, she doesn't argue. It's as if she had been waiting for them. On the way, she grabs a bottle, something dark and red. What is it? She doesn't say; they don't ask.

***

With Sid in her arms, Kiara is wondering what to do. Just then, Bingo comes charging towards them. She ties her son to her waist with her dupatta and springs on the horse's back without another thought.

He neighs as she picks up the reins, and they go speeding off towards Garbett.

***

The ambulance is hurrying towards the tracks when Dr Bishnoi suddenly screams, "Stop!"

Aditya turns towards her with alarm. She tells Madhu to reverse and go towards Garbett. "Bingo went that way just now," she says by way of explanation.

He shakes his head. "I didn't see anyone." Dr Bishnoi tells him that as a vet, she has spent years learning how to communicate with animals and has cultivated a deep connection with them. "It's my special gift. And just now, I felt a message from Bingo. He wants us to follow him." Madhu doesn't argue, having seen her with the maddened horse earlier.

But before they can turn, they hear a galloping sound. Minutes later, a horse carriage draws up alongside them. Rahim chacha is driving, with Tembe, Suman and Todkar at the back. Todkar doesn't seem surprised to see them. He doesn't even ask questions and simply says, "We have to go up to Garbett." His tone is quite urgent.

Madhu tells him that they are going up there too and he notes that an ambulance is better than a horse carriage. "Jump in," Madhu offers. While Suman and Todkar squeeze into the back, Tembe takes the front seat. He looks expressionlessly at the corpse for a moment before instructing Rahim to wait at the junction. No one asks for explanations. Everyone is listening to their own inner voice.

***

Bingo has reached the top of Garbett Point. As he comes to a halt in front of the signboard, Kiara gets off with a big jump. The mountain slopes down into the ravines.

Sid is stirring against her. She unties the dupatta and holds him in her arms. For a moment, he seems almost at ease—protected in his mother's tight embrace. But Kiara can sense disturbance in the air and knows that the time for the final confrontation has come.

***

Dr Bishnoi knows it too. Still in the ambulance, she murmurs, "If only there was someone to help us. Someone close to Shahnaz. Someone she still loves."

"That would be Amit sahab, her husband," Suman replies, remembering how she and Suresh had brought Shahnaz back to the lodge while the young woman still held the remains of her baby. Miraculously, no one had spotted them, given the lateness of the hour. Upon reaching home, Shahnaz disappeared with the cradle in the warehouse above. "She didn't eat or sleep. Just sat there rocking her dead child and calling for Amit. We heard her, but no one dared to go up. We were anticipating the railway officers dropping by any day to inquire about the baby's death on the tracks but no one came," she recalls.

A few days later, however, Amit did turn up at the lodge, eager to see his wife and son. The last few months had been the hardest he had ever endured—isolation at sea, crew replacement restrictions, route and port closures abroad, flight cancellations, and strict quarantine restrictions when he finally reached Indian shores. All the while, he had been worrying about his wife and his son and grieving the loss of his only parent.

"It broke our hearts to tell him all that had happened in the last one year. Learning the circumstances of his son's death filled him with horror, and he broke down like one who had lost everything. We realised that there was no use revealing the truth about Joshi's death. It would have added to his misery. Or worse, he might not have believed it and suspected us of wrongdoings. When we pointed to the door which Shahnaz had barricaded with the bookcase in the library, he insisted on going up to the warehouse. We warned him that the sight would be devastating, but he was determined to be with his wife and convince her of his commitment to her," Suman's voice breaks. Aditya remembers his visit to the warehouse and shudders.

When an overcome Suman can't continue, Madhu takes the narration forward. The warehouse was so filthy and its air so putrid that Amit struggled to step inside. When he finally looked down at the cradle, where his dead baby lay, he vomited immediately. And from a dark corner, Shahnaz crept up to him with a butcher's knife in her hand. The very room had once been her playroom.

As she lunged at him, he turned. In the scuffle that followed, with Amit trying to stop her, the knife went deep into her abdomen. He yelled for the others' help but by the time they reached the spot, she was lying dead on the floor in a pool of blood.

"What happened to him then?" Aditya asks.

"We left him there and rushed out of the room. We decided that enough deaths had happened. The situation had spiralled out of our control and we needed to go to the cops."

"And did you?" prods Aditya.

Shaking her head, Suman tells him that when all of them, along with Khan, Suresh and Rahim, returned to the warehouse to speak to Amit, there was no person or body there except Shahnaz's congealed blood on the floor. "We don't know what happened or where he went. When he didn't return for several days, we shut down the warehouse and stopped showing up for work, telling people that Amit sahab had left for his hometown with his family. Since the wedding had been kept secret from his family, I don't think Amit sahab ever told his friends or relatives about Shahnaz and the baby. At least, none of his folks ever turned up in Matheran asking after him. After Irani sahab's death, the lodge passed on to his brother, as per the will, with a large sum of money set aside for Shahnaz, which remains unclaimed till date. The family assumed that she moved away with her husband sometime after her father's death and we never corrected them. They did come by one day to make inspections and put Cecil up for sale. Thankfully, they were unaware of the warehouse's existence and the dark secret it harboured," explains Suman.

She and the others spread rumours of Shahnaz's *bhoot* to keep buyers away from the property. As Covid raged with more severity, real estate faced a massive toll. Concerned about the plummeting prices and uncertainties around the pandemic's longevity as well as the empty lodge falling into decay, or worse, the hands of mischievous elements, Irani sahab's brother was motivated to make a quick sale.

"And I bought it, thinking I had got a bargain," Aditya sighs.

"Soon rumours of her ghost haunting the property turned true. As long as no one disturbed her home, she didn't harm anyone. But the presence of your little son stirred her to action. She won't rest until she has him," adds Suman.

***

Up in Garbett, Kiara clutches Sid, who is awake now. Shahnaz is standing at the edge of the mountain, asking her to give her Parzaan back.

Kiara holds him tighter. "He's not your son. He's my Sid. My son, Siddharth. Your Parzaan is dead. You killed him."

"No," Shahnaz screams. "My child is alive. You have him."

Just then, with a volley of barks, Google runs up to Kiara, jumping up to lick Sid. Shahnaz points to the puppy, saying, "See? That's our dog. Amit brought him home one day for our unborn child. And after he was born, Joy never left Parzaan's side. Look at him giddy with happiness to be with his playmate again."

"He is not Joy. He's Google," Sid corrects her in a weak voice just as a tall man steps out of the shadows. His face is largely hidden underneath a thick cloud of beard and moustache and his hair falls down to his shoulders. Clad in dirty clothes and with eyes sad and lost, he says, "She's right, Shahnaz. That's not our Parzaan. He's calling out to us. Can't you hear him?"

She does hear it—Parzaan's last cry before the train snuffed the life out of him.

She nods vigorously with tears in her eyes. "Yes, yes. I can. But why won't my baby come to me? I have been calling him for so long."

She then turns to Kiara holding a whimpering Sid and snarls, "She's taken him. That's why Parzaan won't come to me."

The ambulance has reached the top. Aditya is about to jump out, but Dr Bishnoi stops him, saying, "Wait. Amit is here. I had hoped Google would hear me and bring him and he has. Shahnaz is a psychotic spirit, but she loved him deeply once. He is the father of the child she killed and then tried to get back by taking possession of Kiara's body to catch hold of Sid. Meanwhile, your little boy drew Parzaan's lonely spirit to himself with his innocent playfulness."

She adds, "Spirits can penetrate into our hearts and present themselves to us in appealing forms. Sid probably saw Parzaan as a boy of his age—a playmate. Now, if anyone can lead Shahnaz away from the mortals towards the immortals in the desperate search for her son, it's Amit. As a restless spirit, she haunts the living because she has no place among the dead. That's why she can't sense the presence of Parzaan's spirit around her."

There is a sudden flash of lightning and they see Amit walk up to Shahnaz. Parzaan's spirit, a little baby that can barely stand up, is by his side but she doesn't see it yet. He stretches forward his hand to his wife, softly saying, "Come with us. We will be a family again."

At that moment, Dr Bishnoi walks out of the ambulance to persuade Shahnaz. "Go with them. Your son needs you. Your husband needs you. And Sid needs his mother, Kiara, and his father, Aditya. There's nothing more heartbreaking than losing a child. You know that better than anyone, don't you? Give her child back to Kiara. You will never get to Parzaan through Kiara's body. He won't recognise you and you won't recognise him. And Sid, even when comatose, knew that you weren't his mamma, and so your powers couldn't control him fully."

Shahnaz is unconvinced. She snarls at Dr Bishnoi and moves towards Kiara, saying, "I will get him. I will."

But Amit comes in the way. Holding out his hand again, he says, "Come, let's live the dream we once saw."

She looks at him tentatively. The sincerity on his face stirs the deep impression his companionship had made on her soul while she was still alive. Desperate for that same love and safety, she impulsively reaches for his hand. At that moment, both Shahnaz and Parzaan's spirits enter Amit's body, taking possession of him, and he jumps into the ravines.

Aditya runs to Kiara and Sid and takes them in his arms.

"I hope Shahnaz doesn't come back. If she does, you must stop her. I am going to Sumeila," Suman tells Madhu.

He and Dr Bishnoi look at each other and smile. They have vanquished a disruptive spirit.

Rahim chacha comes up in the horse carriage. He sees Bingo standing there wild-eyed, foaming at the mouth, and runs up to him. Holding the horse's head and looking into his eyes like Dr Bishnoi had, he quietly says, "I don't know if you are dead or alive, but you are still my son. I was there when you came into the world, and I should have never given you away. Well, now you are coming home with me."

As they all move towards the ambulance, Sid looks around, wondering where Google has disappeared again.

"He was Parzaan's dog and he went with him. Once we get back to Mumbai, I will get you one just like him," says Aditya.

The boy smiles.

The cops offer to drop the Malhotras off at the lodge, in case they want to spend the night there. Aditya shakes his head, "No, that is Shahnaz's home. It will always be hers. We are going to our home in Mumbai."

Todkar nods. "We are also going back to Mumbai. Come, we will go together to Dasturi. Rahim chacha can drop us there once he has settled Bingo."

Madhu tells them that Suman and he will take Khan chacha's body back home to his wife and daughter.

As the Malhotras, with the two cops and the doctor, leave Matheran, the skies clear. The moon comes out. Rahim chacha points to it and says, "Look, it's a blood moon."

Epilogue

Three months later.

Kaira and Aditya have just discovered that she is pregnant. Although the good news thrills them both, Kiara ardently hopes that her second pregnancy won't be as complicated as her first. At least Sid will never be lonely now, she sighs peacefully.

The ecstatic little boy calls up Sara and Sana and exclaims, "Now, we will be two too, just like you both."

They laugh and he adds, "If I get a brother—and I know I will—I am going to call him Parzaan. He will be my friend for life."

This time they don't laugh. But the dog by Sid's side yaps and wags his tail in agreement. His name is Google.

***

Amit's body has been found in the ravines, and the news channels' speculations are going into an overdrive. "One more tourist has died in an accidental death in Matheran. He must have fallen off his horse since he wasn't wearing a helmet or any other proper gear. These deaths need to be investigated properly, but the cops' lackadaisical attitude..."

Listening to the news, Tembe says, "If only they knew the truth."

Todkar cautions him. "Shhh, even walls have ears."

Just then, his wife Shanti enters the room with a platter of pakoras, grousing, "Ever since you returned from Matheran the second time, both of you keep whispering to each other. Tell me your secret too, na?"

Todkar looks at his deputy and smiles. "Shanti, Tembe here wants to get married and he is looking for a girl just like you. He has even decided to go to Matheran for his honeymoon. Can you help him?"

Tembe splutters, almost choking on his tea.

***

Zoya and Jimmy are sitting together in her house. She is cuddling up to him, but his eyes are far away. "Guess what, Jimmy! I bought a house." She giggles.

He turns to her in surprise. "You bought a house?"

She nods excitedly, reminding him that she has come into a lot of money left to her by her grandparents who passed away in a tragic car accident soon after their return from Matheran.

"You spent all that money on an apartment in Mumbai? That was silly," he reprimands her.

She shakes her head, snapping, "I'm not dumb! No, I bought a place in Matheran. It was a distress sale, and I got the property dirt cheap."

She jumps up and twirls before him. "I am now the new owner of Cecil Lodge. The next time we are there in Matheran, we won't have to stay in a rundown lodge where they find dead bodies in the pool. We will live in our own lodge. Now that Covid is no longer an international emergency and travel restrictions have been lifted, I am going to get it all spruced up and open it to guests early next year."

Jimmy can only say, "Congratulations," before she locks lips with him, her eyes glittering black.

***

In the hospital, Priya continues to lie listlessly in bed. Her condition hasn't changed. She is still comatose.

Amar, who is sitting by her bedside, tells her that one day soon, they will all go back to Matheran because that's where the root of her illness lies. "You will get well and I will reunite you with Jimmy because that's the only way I will get my Zoya back. By the way, she has..." The nurse comes in to remind him that visiting hours are up.

He nods and leans down to whisper to Priya. "she has bought a lodge. Cecil Lodge."

***

In Matheran, Suman, who has moved in with the Khans, has just come back from the market with Shazia. "Guess what we just heard! Aditya sahab has sold Cecil," she exclaims.

Sumeila is playing carrom with her grandson Bilal and nods approvingly. "That's a wise decision. It's not safe."

Her daughter interjects, "But someone else has bought it, and I hear they will be opening it up for business."

Bilal looks up from the game excitedly. "That's great. Ammi, why don't you get a job there? Then I can play on its grounds. It has a badminton court, merry-go-round and..."

A loud "no" spoken in unison by the three women makes him stare at them curiously. His grandmother, mother and

Suman chachi are all looking really upset. But never mind, he thinks. Once it opens, he will sneak in there. He has heard that they even have a foosball board that can be cranked up.

***

Rahim is feeding Bingo. The horse is getting better, but they still don't let tourists ride him. Only he or Rashid can take him out for a run. With them, he is docile. But even now, on certain nights, he gets jittery and difficult to control.

***

Madhu rushes in looking upset. "Have you heard the news?" Rahim is surprised to see him.

"You're back? I thought you were in Karjat."

Madhu nods but says that when he heard the news, he had to come back and warn everyone. "Someone has bought Cecil Lodge again."

Bingo lifts its front legs and neighs.

***

Dr Bishnoi is sitting on her terrace. Hari puts a tray of lemons and sindoor before her and leaves. She has a new case. She slices a *nimboo* and sprinkles some vermillion on it. The red powder turns black.

Frowning, she picks up the lemon slice and looks into it. Shahnaz snarls back.

Trembling, she throws the lemon away and murmurs, "The spirit is rising again."

Acknowledgements

I've always had a keen connection with the written word, having written the screenplays for all my movies thus far. It was Karan Johar who helped me make this a part of my world with his sage advice that if one wants to tell a story, one must be able to write it as well. To him, I remain indebted for many good things in my career.

Writing a novel, though, wasn't even on my wish list until a couple of years ago. It was right at the cusp of COVID-19's outbreak that I was tasked with a rather interesting assignment for an online learning app: conceptualizing, directing and shooting ten celebrities across various fields as they taught viewers the nuances of their craft. Actor Manoj Bajpai, tennis icon Sania Mirza, and comedian Johnny Lever were some of the personalities I worked with. Among them was also world-renowned author Ruskin Bond, who taught 'How to Become an Author'. It was a privilege to work with him closely and witness his life in the magical hills of Mussoorie. That even in his eighties he continued to write as brilliantly and prolifically helped me realize that a writer never grows old. I owe a debt of gratitude to him. I decided that I too would try my hand at writing a novel, thereby applying my storytelling and writing skills in a different medium.

If only I knew that the opportunity would present itself soon after. As the first lockdown was imposed to curb the pandemic's spread, I started writing a horror story, intertwining my childhood memories of staying at my favourite hotel in Matheran with paranormal and spiritual experiences later in life as an adult. *Blood Moon* has resulted from a marriage between lived experiences and imagination, fact and fancy…

My thanks to Soumya Duggal of Om Books International for expertly guiding the edits on the book and ironing out its rough edges. A word of gratitude for The Book Bakers for putting me in touch with Om Books International, where the publisher, Ajay Mago, and the editor-in-chief, Shantanu Ray Chaudhuri, have been instrumental in this book coming together. A big thank you to my friend Roshmilla Bhattacharya for her unconditional support.

Finally, I'd like to dedicate this novel to those who still people my fond childhood memories of staying at Cecil Hotel. The late Yezdi Irani, my dear friend and the then-owner of the heritage hotel, with whom I spent numerous moments exploring this lovely property. His wife, Shehnaz, and his mother, Meena Aunty, and their most loving hotel staff: Madhu, Shivaji, Balu, Ashok and many more. Suresh ghodawallah was our man who accompanied us on delightful early morning rides. My dear family and friends who were all part of these trips and still love Matheran. Shilpa Kadam, my dearest friend whom I recently lost to illness, was my constant companion in Matheran and is forever etched in my memory.